Dear Reader,

When I was asked to write a fairy tale with a twist, I jumped at the opportunity. What a challenge— and what fun! As I considered what fairy tale I wanted to write, Cinderella's stepsisters leaped into my mind. It couldn't have been easy, having the wicked stepmother as their mother. I wanted to know more about them, to create a story where they watched Cinderella be the belle of the ball, but maybe Prince Charming had the wrong sister? Updating the story to modern times, social media included, added to both the fun and the challenge. I hope you enjoy my twist on a classic story, and fall in love alongside Alessandro and Liane.

Happy reading,

Kate

After spending three years as a die-hard New Yorker, **Kate Hewitt** now lives in a small village in the English Lake District with her husband, their five children and a golden retriever. In addition to writing intensely emotional stories, she loves reading, baking and playing chess with her son— she has yet to win against him, but she continues to try. Learn more about Kate at kate-hewitt.com.

Books by Kate Hewitt

Harlequin Presents

Claiming My Bride of Convenience
Vows to Save His Crown
Pride & the Italian's Proposal

One Night with Consequences

Princess's Nine-Month Secret
Greek's Baby of Redemption

Secret Heirs of Billionaires

The Secret Kept from the Italian
The Italian's Unexpected Baby

Visit the Author Profile page
at Harlequin.com for more titles.

Kate Hewitt

A SCANDAL MADE
AT MIDNIGHT

HARLEQUIN
PRESENTS

HARLEQUIN®

PRESENTS™

Recycling programs
for this product may
not exist in your area.

ISBN-13: 978-1-335-73849-3

A Scandal Made at Midnight

For questions and comments about the quality of this book,
please contact us at CustomerService@Harlequin.com.

Harlequin Enterprises ULC
22 Adelaide St. West, 41st Floor
Toronto, Ontario M5H 4E3, Canada
www.Harlequin.com

Printed in U.S.A.

A SCANDAL MADE
AT MIDNIGHT

CHAPTER ONE

'AREN'T THEY THE most incredible things you've seen?'

Liane Blanchard gave a rueful laugh of acknowledgement as Ella twirled around, blonde curls flying, her musical peal of laughter echoing through the living room, its windows open to the summery breeze wafting in from Central Park.

'That's certainly one word for them,' she replied with a smile. With five-inch platform heels, encrusted with diamantes and made entirely of glass, the shoes really were incredible. They also looked painful and potentially impossible to wear, not that either of those, Liane knew, would put Ella off for a second. 'You're wearing them to the ball, I presume?'

'Of course. I've got quite a plan for these shoes, as it happens.' Ella winked as she slipped the shoes off, replacing them in the layers of tissue paper in the silver shoe box that came from one of Manhattan's up-and-coming fashion designers. As a self-made social media influencer, Ella was often getting samples from desperate designers who longed to be the next big thing, just as she did. 'You should see the dress I'm wearing. It goes *perfectly* with the shoes.'

'Not made of glass, I hope?' Liane joked, only to have Ella give her another wink.

'No, but the fabric version of it! But don't worry, don't worry.' She held up one hand as she shook back her long, tumbling blonde hair. 'It's perfectly decent. Not *too* see-through.' She giggled while Liane smiled and shook her head wryly. Ella was twenty-two, gorgeous, and as happy and carefree as a lark. At twenty-seven innately quiet and cautious, Liane sometimes felt like she was the only thing keeping her younger stepsister from falling headlong into disaster—or at least chaos—again and again.

'What a ridiculous pair of shoes.'

Along with her mother, Liane amended silently. Amelie Ash stood in the doorway of the living room, tall, grey-haired and unsmiling as she looked down her long thin nose at the ridiculous shoes Ella had just put back in the box.

'They are ridiculous, aren't they?' she agreed cheerfully as she put the lid back on the box. 'That's the point.'

Liane had always admired the way Ella refused to let her stepmother get her down. They'd blended their families when Ella had only been six, a cherubic little girl with rosy cheeks and candy floss curls. Amelie, the mother of two awkward preteen girls at the time, had not taken to her at all.

It hadn't helped that her new husband, Robert Ash, had loved to lavish presents and attention on his only child, since her mother had died when Ella was just a baby. And yet even though Ella had certainly been indulged by her father, Liane reflected with affection, she hadn't actually been *spoiled*. At least not too much. She was simply high-spirited, full of fun—and the complete opposite of her stepmother—as well as Liane—in every way.

'Where on earth are you wearing them?' Amelie asked with a sniff.

'To the ball, of course!'

Liane tensed instinctively as her mother's face became pinched, her cold grey eyes narrowing, lips pursing like a particularly withered prune. She knew that look, had seen it many times over the years as life—as well as her daughters—had continued to disappoint her mother, and she'd done her best to mitigate against it, placate and persevere and please, usually to little avail.

'The ball?' Amelie repeated icily. 'Ella, my dear, you are not going to the ball. You weren't invited.'

For the merest second Ella's laughing expression faltered, and her china blue eyes widened as she shot Liane an uncertain, questioning look.

'No, she wasn't invited,' Liane interjected quickly, 'but she's coming as my guest. I checked with the assistant handling the RSVPs, and plus ones are allowed.' She could have never gone otherwise, knowing Ella would have to stay at home. She'd offered to give Ella her own invitation, as she wasn't much of a one for parties, but Ella had insisted they go together.

Her mother's lips thinned. Liane knew she would much rather Ella didn't attend what was billed to be *the* event of the season—a ball hosted by the notoriously reclusive hotel magnate Alessandro Rossi, to celebrate a hundred years of his family's luxury hotels, for the crème de la crème of New York society. Not that they could actually count themselves one of that number, but Liane's father, Michel Blanchard, had been a minor diplomat and a casual acquaintance of Alessandro Rossi's father, Leonardo, a long time ago. Liane had been as shocked as anyone when the invitation on thick, creamy card had been slotted through their letter box, although her mother had been smugly exultant.

'Of course we'd be invited,' she'd scoffed, preening. 'Your father was a dear friend of Leonardo Rossi's. You know how he lent him money when he needed it.'

A hundred francs at a casino, thirty years ago, hardly the lofty business deal her mother made it seem. Of course Liane did not say any of this. She had long ago learned to hold her tongue around her mother; it made everything easier for everyone if she placated rather than poured oil onto the flames of her mother's ire.

In any case, she was looking forward to going to the ball, admittedly with some apprehension; as a French teacher working at a girls' school on the Upper East Side, she'd chosen to live a quiet life with her mother and sisters, rather than step into the spotlight that Ella launched herself into, again and again, in pursuit of fame and fortune. Liane had no interest in either; the losses she'd experienced in life had taught her to be cautious, to stick to the shadows. When you didn't, you got hurt. She'd seen it with her father, she felt it with her mother. Putting yourself out there could hurt, and Liane had decided long ago that she'd rather not even try.

But, she thought as Ella put the shoe box away, attending a ball would certainly be a nice change, even if she knew she would stay on the sidelines as she always did.

'I doubt you have anything appropriate to wear,' Amelie remarked with another sniff as her stepdaughter came back into the living room. Ella might own the house they all lived in, given to her by her father with the proviso that her stepmother and sisters could live in it for all their lives, but otherwise she did not have a penny to her name and was dependent on her stepmother's grudging generosity.

'Oh, but I do,' Ella replied sweetly. 'A fashion designer friend of mine has made the most glorious gown—don't worry, Belle-Mère, I promise I won't embarrass you by wearing rags.'

Which was hardly her mother's concern, Liane knew. No, her mother's concern was quite the opposite—that gorgeous, laughing Ella would show her and her sister Manon up, which she undoubtedly would, without even trying. Liane was used to it, Manon didn't really care, and her mother became coldly, quietly infuriated. She had aspirations of her daughters marrying wealthy, well-connected men, the kind of men who would be guests at the Rossi Ball. Liane couldn't see it happening herself. She'd be afraid to say boo to a man like that, if truth were told, while Ella could turn flirting into a competitive sport.

'How fortunate for you,' Amelie stated coldly.

'Liane? Has your dress come back from the seamstress?'

'Yes, I picked it up this morning.' Liane forced a smile even though she partly dreaded wearing that old blue bag of a dress—a castoff of her mother's, hardly flattering, yet all they could afford.

'And just in time too, considering the ball is tomorrow night,' her mother replied, and, with another narrowed look of dislike for her stepdaughter, Amelie stalked out of the room. Liane gave her sister a sympathetic look.

'Don't mind her.'

'I never do,' Ella assured her sunnily. 'But you haven't shown me your dress. Let's see it.'

'It's nothing much—' Liane said hurriedly, knowing what an awful understatement her words were.

'Oh, come on, Liane! I bet you'll look amazing in it. Show me?'

'Very well.' She never could resist her sister's puppy dog eyes. 'But it really isn't much at all.' With a sigh she headed upstairs, Ella following her to her bedroom on the first floor, its long sash windows facing the house's narrow back garden, Central Park visible in the distance. Ella had the small room at the top of the house by her stepmother's decree, but she had always insisted she didn't mind.

'More privacy,' she'd assured Liane when she'd offered to switch. 'And you know what a night owl I am. I'd hate to disturb everyone with my noise.' Liane still felt guilty. Ella had been short-changed in so many ways since her father's death three years ago, but she never put up a fuss, no matter how her stepmother tried to limit her life.

'Now show me this dress,' Ella commanded as Liane reached for the plastic-swathed gown hanging from her wardrobe door. 'I hope it's sensational.'

'Nothing like yours, I'm sure.' Liane eased the plastic off the gown. Her mother might have pretensions of her and Manon catching the attention of an eligible man like Alessandro Rossi, but their limited budget did not stretch to ball gowns that would serve such a purpose.

The powder-blue dress had been her mother's and a local seamstress had updated its debatably classic look. Amelie had insisted it was still in style, but Liane had her doubts. So did Ella.

'Thank goodness you got rid of the ruffles,' she said as she eyed it critically. 'Otherwise it would have been pure nineteen-eighties, and not in a good way, unfortunately.'

'I know.' Liane suppressed a sigh. She was used to looking like a wallflower, with her pale, washed-out looks—or so her mother said—but wearing a forty-year-old dress took even that to its limits. 'I don't really mind. I'm not one for parties anyway, Ella, you know that. And no one will be looking at me anyway, I'm quite sure.'

'Still, this is *the* party of the year,' Ella protested. Liane couldn't help but notice she didn't even argue her second point. 'You can't wear something you could find in a thrift shop.'

'Ouch.' Liane pretended to wince. There was too much truth in her sister's words. Even with the seamstress's help the dress looked far too dated and worn, bagging about her bosom and hips, the material possessing the unlovely sheen of cheap satin. But what did it really matter? As she'd said and Ella had silently agreed, no one would be looking at her. They'd all be looking at Ella, and she was glad of it.

'Look, you can't wear this,' Ella declared as she slid her phone out of her pocket. 'Not to this party. It might be fine for Manon—she really doesn't care about dresses—'

'She's wearing black, as she always does.' Manon loved her work as an administrative assistant in a law office and couldn't care less about fashion or finding a husband. She was only going because their mother had absolutely insisted and, as they both knew when it came to their mother's machinations, it was easier to go along than to resist. Easier to stay silent than protest against her constant barrage of criticism, because her daughters disappointed her as much as her husbands had.

'Of course she is. Let me text my designer friend. I think she was working on another gown, and it would be perfect for you. Violet to match your eyes.'

'Oh, I don't know,' Liane protested, not wanting Ella to go to such trouble.

'I'm telling you it would be perfect—'

'I'm not wearing something transparent,' Liane warned her.

'Of course not,' Ella answered with a laugh as her fingers flew over her phone. 'That one's for me. Trust me, Liane, it really will be perfect. You'll be the belle of the ball!'

'Hardly,' Liane returned. 'That's a position reserved for you.' Ella took to the spotlight naturally, and always had, much to Amelie Ash's ire. Liane knew their mother had always wanted her and Manon to be more like Ella, sparkling and sociable and charismatic, even as she'd disdained and even despised her stepdaughter for being exactly how she was. As for herself? She'd be happy enough to stand unnoticed on the sidelines as she watched Ella take the world by storm. Still, she decided with a smile, she was feminine enough to feel it would be nice to wear a pretty dress while she was doing it.

The party was in full swing as Alessandro Rossi stepped out of the elevator onto the penthouse floor of Hotel Rossi, his family empire's flagship hotel in the centre of Manhattan. From the open doors of the ballroom he heard the tinkle of laughter and crystal, the strains of the seventeen-piece orchestra. All around him the city stretched out, a carpet of darkness lit by the golden blur of streetlights, matched by the glitter and sparkle of crystal chandeliers and champagne flutes, not to mention the hundreds of thousands of dollars' worth of jewels dripping off most of the women in the room. The Rossi Ball, the first of its kind, had been hyped to be the event of the year in the city, as it had to be. The publicity was the only reason he was having this tedious affair in the first place.

Straightening his black tie, his eyes narrowing as his hooded grey gaze swept the crowded room, Alessandro stepped into the ballroom—and then froze when he heard a tiny strangled yelp. *What the...?*

'I'm so sorry,' a woman said. Her voice was soft, with a gentle trace of a French accent. 'I didn't mean to get in your way. I do apologise.'

Considering he'd stepped on *her* foot, he had a feeling he was the one who'd got in the way. He hadn't even seen her. Alessandro's eyes narrowed as he glanced down at the woman in question—barely coming to his shoulder, with white-blonde hair piled on top of her head and a small, slender figure encased in swathes of gauzy violet. She was standing behind a potted palm by the door, which was why he hadn't seen her. That, and because she was also rather petite. She tilted her head back to gaze up at him with eyes the same colour as her dress as she tried not to wince. She was, he realised, hopping on one foot.

'I apologise. I hope I didn't break your toes?' He'd meant to sound charmingly wry, but the woman gave him a level look.

'Only my pinkie toe, which I can live without, although I might walk with a limp from now on. Don't you need pinkie toes for balance?' She spoke so sombrely that for a horrified split second he thought she was serious—and then her smile emerged, reminding Alessandro bizarrely of a cuckoo clock—it popped out and then it was gone, and it left him smiling in return, strangely lightened.

'I thought you were serious,' he told her.

'I think I am.' Again with the glimpse of a smile, so fleeting and precious, making something long dead flicker inside him, come to life. 'But don't worry, I'll live. Clearly this is a punishment for my pride. I shouldn't have let my sister convince me to wear these ridiculous shoes.'

Alessandro's mouth quirked. 'It's been my experience that most women wear ridiculous shoes.'

'What an insulting generalisation.' She wasn't laughing but it felt like she was, and it made him want to laugh as well. *Strange.* He generally wasn't one for levity. 'I assure you I am the proud owner of several pairs of sensible shoes, and not one even slightly ridiculous pair.'

He nodded towards her feet. 'Excluding these.'

'These belong to my sister.' She reached down to lift the hem of her gown to show him the shoes in question, along with a pair of slim ankles. The shoes were stiletto-heeled and dyed violet to match the dress. 'Truly ridiculous,' she proclaimed with another smile, this one reaching her eyes.

Alessandro had certainly seen more ridiculous shoes in his time, but he decided not to say as much. As reluctantly charmed as he was by this funny, elfin woman, and as much he had an odd longing to prolong the conversation, he needed to begin the tedious and unpleasant business of meeting and greeting his guests, get the necessary publicity photos and then make a strategic retreat. Focus on the task at hand, as he always did, with resolve and determination. No distractions, no temptations, nothing to deter or derail him from his chosen course.

'Very fetching, I'm sure,' he told her, his tone instinctively several degrees cooler than it had been previously.

He watched, feeling an inexplicable sense of loss, as a shuttered look came over her face, like a curtain coming down, all the light and sparkle suddenly gone. She let go of her dress so the hem hid her feet, the gauzy material brushing the floor. 'Thank you, indeed. Clearly I've already taken up too much of your time. I do apologise.'

Before he could reply, she took a step back and then another, the crowd swallowing her up within seconds while he simply stared. Strange woman. *Beguiling* woman. No, he told himself, just strange. And rather mousy, really, with all that pale hair and skin. Colourless, although her eyes had been extraordinary, like amethysts…

He gave himself a mental shake as he turned back to the ballroom. He needed to stop thinking about some nobody woman who would do nothing to further his cause. The only reason he was here was to generate positive publicity for the Rossi brand—a prospect that filled him with both determination and ire.

He hadn't realised when he'd taken over as CEO of the sprawling family empire from his father last year just how much the hotel side of the business had started to falter. Leonardo Rossi had seconded his son to Rome for ten years, to oversee their European assets and investments, the main source of the Rossi wealth. While Alessandro had been solidifying their financial business, his father, no doubt too busy with his latest *amour*, had let the hotel empire's flagship hotel in

America run nearly into the ground, simply through mismanagement and indifference. It was stunts like this one that were supposedly going to save it, according to the consultant Alessandro had hired.

'The Rossi brand has become associated with stuffy, old world gentility,' the branding specialist, a woman who barely looked out of grad school, had told him bluntly several months ago, when Alessandro had flown into New York to find the flagship hotel only half full at one of the busiest times of the year. 'At least in America. People want to stay somewhere exciting and cutting edge, somewhere young and new.'

'The Rossi brand is over a hundred years old,' Alessandro had pointed out dryly. 'We are never going to be young and new.'

'Which is why it's time for a reinvention.'

Initially he'd been against the whole idea. Rossi hotels were the best in the world—the epitome of elegance, luxury, class. They did not need reinventing, and the last thing he wanted to do was to chase after a fleeting trend. The Rossi name was built on the idea of stable dependability; the world around might change, but its timeless elegance and luxury did not.

And yet, as he'd toured the New York hotel, he'd realised *something* needed to change. Rooms were empty. Guests were mainly octogenarians. The branding consultant, he'd been forced to concede reluctantly, might have had a point. He could turn around his family's fortunes just as he'd done with their investments, but it might need a different approach.

What he realised was he didn't want to change anything about the hotels—they were still timelessly stylish and luxurious, an oasis of peace in a bustling city. What he needed to do was simply change how they were perceived. Hence this party, along with several others over the next few weeks, each one at a different Rossi hotel, with him in attendance, showing how *fun* he was, which was, he knew, something of a joke. He wasn't fun at all. He didn't want to be. Fun was for layabouts and useless charmers, people who skated through life by other people's hard work, tumbling in and out of love because they were led by their emotions, capricious as those could be, and caused pain and suffering in their wake. People like his father. That was not who he was at all, who he'd chosen to be, but for tonight, as well as for a few others, for expediency's sake, the camera could lie.

He moved through the crowds, offering brief smiles to anyone whose eyes he met, stopping to make idle chitchat with whoever waylaid him. Several of the glossier gossip magazines were here, discreetly taking their paparazzi shots. Alessandro made sure to pause and pose as needed, his relaxed smile hiding his gritted teeth, the tension that was twanging through his whole body.

He hated parties. *Hated* them. Had despised them since he'd been about three years old and had been trotted out as a prop for his parents to show their marriage wasn't the train wreck everyone knew it to be, paraded around like some sort of show monkey. Just the memory made an icy sweat prickle on the back of his neck, his stomach clench with remembered anxiety he'd long ago forced himself to move past. Their pathetic little stunt had never worked, but still they'd tried. Over and over again. It had given him a decided aversion to socialising of any kind…as well as marriage.

As he took a sip of champagne, he aimed a discreet glance at his watch. How long would he have to socialise, showing everyone the obvious—that Rossi hotels were the best in the world? And yes, they were *fun*.

'Of course,' the branding consultant had told him at that meeting, her smile a bit mischievous, 'what you really need is a representative for the hotel—someone young and fun and cool who comes to all these parties.' She'd given him a pertly expectant look, while Alessandro had merely stared back.

Was she implying she would be up for the job? He wasn't about to hire some wannabe starlet to gush and gallivant about the hotel, however, whatever this well-meaning woman said. 'I cannot imagine who that would be,' he'd told her. 'For the moment I'll settle for a few judicious publicity shots.'

How many had they taken now? Eight, nine? Surely that was enough? He looked down at his watch again. He'd only been here for fifteen minutes. Unbelievable. He already felt both wired and exhausted by the attention, the chitchat, the speculation, *the memories*.

'Here's our little darling boy. Come here, Alessandro, and show everyone how much you love us.'

No matter how many obedient hugs and smiles he'd given, it had never been enough. His mother would drink herself into a stupor, his father would embark on another affair. And they would scream and rage at each other, with him always at the centre, being used.

He'd always vowed he would never let himself be so used again.

He pushed the memories away as he glanced around the ballroom, and it wasn't until his gaze had skated over half the people that he realised who he was looking for. Her. That funny little woman with the purple eyes and the smile that wasn't. He shook his head as if to clear it, and that was when he caught sight of the woman holding court in the centre of the room—and he wondered how he had ever missed her.

She was objectively gorgeous, first of all, with long, tumbling blonde hair, a figure that was both curvaceous and slender, encased in sparkling gauze that made her look like a mermaid, and an almost naked one at that, considering the nearly sheer gauze of her dress. But, beyond her obvious good looks, she had a mesmerising quality about her, something that made it hard to look away. He found himself taking a step towards her, and then another, intrigued by the way she held court in the middle of the room.

She was surrounded by a crowd of admirers, men as well as women, the men discreetly—or not—ogling her figure, the women simply wanting to be in her reflected radiance. She tossed her hair over her shoulder and her cerulean gaze met his for an instant, causing him to hesitate mid-stride. Her eyes widened and her smile curved with a catlike knowledge. She fluttered her eyelashes, but in a way that made it seem like a joke, like she was mocking herself—or him. He kept walking.

From the corner of his eye he saw a flash of violet as a small, svelte figure move quickly out of the way, sidling along the wall. He hesitated, almost turned, compelled by some deeper, instinctive desire to find *that* woman, as different as she was. To see her smile again.

Then he retrained his gaze on the Princess holding court in the middle of the ballroom. *Focus*, as he always did. He would not be guided by emotion but by reason, for here, surely, was the new face of Rossi Hotels.

CHAPTER TWO

LIANE WATCHED ALESSANDRO ROSSI walk towards her sister like a man on a mission. He wouldn't be the first—half the men in the room had already been swept up in her orbit—but he would certainly be the most eligible. She forced herself to quash the tiniest flicker of envy she couldn't keep herself from feeling as he stood in front of Ella, one hand in his pocket, his manner relaxed as he gave her a slow, smiling look.

From her position behind a potted plant Liane could study him unguardedly, taking in his tall, powerful figure, well over six feet. She barely topped five feet herself and standing next to him had made her feel small, but strangely in a good way. Delicate. When he'd gazed down at her she'd felt warmed right through, as if by the sun, as if she'd *swallowed* the sun. Silly to think like that, of course. Most likely he'd simply seen her as an amusement, maybe even an irritation. He'd certainly dismissed her quickly enough.

Besides, he was far more suited to Ella than to her. With his close-cut hair of burnished midnight, those iron-grey eyes and a face that looked as if it had been

sculpted from marble, his classic good looks comple-
mented Ella's blonde goddess-like beauty far more than
Liane's less striking looks.

'You must make more of yourself, Liane,' her mother
often complained. *'You're so pale and mousy, you completely fade away.'*

Once, on her mother's bidding, Liane had tried to do
just that—carefully applying make-up, wearing a nicer
dress to work, putting her hair up in a chignon, adding
earrings and a necklace. She'd felt both shy and hopeful as she'd stepped through the doors of the school.

The results had been, to Liane's mind, disastrous—
or at least humiliating. The receptionist had raised her
eyebrows and smirked. *'Ooh, who are you trying to
impress, then?'* The girls in her class had tittered behind their hands. *'Have you got a date, Miss?'* they'd
asked, shooting each other looks. But worst of all had
been the teachers Liane had overheard gossiping about
her when she'd been in the staffroom, marking papers
in the corner—they hadn't even seen her!

'What on earth has got into Liane? Who is she trying to impress? She looks absolutely ridiculous.'

'There is such a thing as trying too hard, isn't there?'
They'd shared a look as they'd laughed. 'Poor thing. I
suppose she just wants to be noticed for once.'

Liane had shrunk back into her chair, desperate not
to be noticed right then. After the women had left, she'd
gone into the bathroom and scrubbed off all the make-
up. The next day she'd returned to school in her usual
serviceable blouse and skirt, her hair back in a neat
clip, her face devoid of make-up. The receptionist had

given her a pitying look as Liane had marched past, her head held high, determined never to try to be noticed again. There was a reason some people naturally sparkled and shone—and some people didn't. Besides, if you didn't try, you didn't get hurt, and the shadows were a far safer place than the spotlight.

As for the spotlight... Liane turned back to Alessandro Rossi and her sister. They were like Venus and Apollo, she mused, or perhaps Venus and Ares, for there was something almost warlike about Alessandro Rossi's hard profile—the lines of his cheek and jaw were unforgiving, like two slashes of a blade. While Ella was softness and light, Alessandro was all hard, dark planes. Yet together, like two demigods of high society, they worked, that much was obvious, for the whole crowd was watching, cameras snapping, as the orchestra struck up another tune and Alessandro took Ella in his arms.

She was not going to feel jealous, Liane told herself severely, because that would be utterly absurd and frankly shaming. She'd had a few minutes of awkward chitchat with the man, about *shoes*, of all things. Ridiculous shoes. The fact that he made her heart skip a beat and a blush come to her cheeks when she thought about him now meant nothing. Nothing at all, except perhaps that she was completely inexperienced in matters of romance and flirtation, which she already knew perfectly well.

'Ella is the centre of attention, as usual,' Manon remarked sourly as she came to stand beside Liane, moving a palm frond out of the way. 'How does she manage it?'

'She's beautiful and funny and nice. Why wouldn't she?' Liane smiled and shrugged, while her older sister tracked Ella and Alessandro with a frown. 'Don't be jealous,' she entreated quietly. 'She's never spiteful about it, you know.'

'I'm not *jealous*,' Manon replied with a huff. 'I'm just bored. I didn't want to come to this wretched ball in the first place, and Maman has been throwing me at any man under the age of sixty. It's humiliating. Why is she so desperate to see us married off? You'd think it was the eighteen-hundreds or something.'

'She wants to see us provided for, and that's the only way she knows how.' Despite her mother's stern ways and near-constant barrage of criticism, Liane couldn't help but feel a rush of sympathy for her—she'd had two husbands, both of whom had died and left her with little more than pennies. She still managed to eke out an existence of shabby gentility, depending on a few small investments and her reputation to at least give the pretence of gracious living, but it wasn't much, and Ella inheriting the house had been a very bitter pill to swallow. Of course she wanted to see her daughters provided for—and, as she reminded them on many occasions, working as a teacher and a secretary was not adequate provision, not in her view, anyway.

'Why are you two standing in the corner?'

Liane tensed as her mother sailed over, dressed as always in widow's black, a martyr to her disappointments for ever. She eyed Liane critically. 'I don't think purple suits you. The blue would have been better.'

Manon rolled her eyes. 'The blue was terrible, Maman.'

Amelie sniffed. 'I suppose Ella gave you that dress?'

'Just to borrow.' As usual Liane felt the need to smooth things over. 'I'll wear the blue next time, Maman.' There probably wouldn't be a next time; it wasn't as if she went to balls every day of the week.

Amelie turned, her eyes narrowing as she took in the sight of Ella and Alessandro together. 'Making a spectacle of herself as usual, I see.' She poked Liane between her shoulder blades. 'Why don't you go over and say something? I saw you talking with Rossi earlier, so you've made his acquaintance.'

'Only because he stepped on my foot…!'

'Well, say hello again, then.' Amelie poked her again, hard enough that Liane was forced to take a few steps towards Ella and Alessandro.

'Maman…' she whispered, horrified, while Manon smothered a laugh.

'Yes, do go over, Liane,' she chimed in. 'I'm sure they'll both appreciate it.'

Amelie nudged her again, so Liane found herself standing alone on the edge of the dance floor, frozen in embarrassment. People were looking at her, sensing that something was going on, waiting to see what she would do.

'Go on, Liane!' Amelie barked, loud enough for people nearby to hear.

Liane closed her eyes. Why did her mother have to be so pushy? And why did she let herself be pushed?

'Are you hoping to cut in?'

Her eyes flew open as, mortified, she saw Alessandro and Ella standing before her. Oh, no...

'I...' The syllable came out in a squeak. Alessandro looked bemused, Ella sympathetic.

'Yes, go on and dance, Liane. I'd like to sit down for a bit.' As easily as she did everything, Ella drew her by the hand towards Alessandro. Before Liane even knew what was happening, Alessandro had taken her in his arms and Ella had disappeared. A pity dance, she thought miserably. How awful. Yet even so she couldn't keep from being affected by the citrusy tang of his aftershave, the muscles bunching his arm as she rested one hand on his shoulder, and his hand spanned the dip of her waist, warm and heavy.

'You know Ella?' Alessandro asked as he gazed down at her, moving her about the floor with grace and ease while Liane did her best to keep up.

'Yes, she's my sister.'

'How surprising. You two are nothing alike.'

A flush came to her cheeks at the implied criticism. Of course she already knew she was nothing like Ella. 'We're stepsisters, actually.'

'Ah, I see.'

His knowing tone both annoyed and hurt her. Why did *everyone* have to see her as someone less than? She wasn't envious of Ella, but she was so very tired of not being appreciated for herself—someone who didn't crave the spotlight. What was so wrong with that?

'The two of you look very well together,' Liane remarked, a touch of acid to her tone. 'The belle and beau of the ball.'

'You think so?' Alessandro looked only amused. 'Then why did you cut in?'

Colour washed her cheeks. 'I did not!'

'You seemed as if you were about to.'

She was not going to admit that her mother had pushed her onto the dance floor. 'I was just trying to get Ella's attention,' she improvised stiffly. 'My mother wanted to speak to her.'

'Ah, well, then, why didn't you say so?'

'I didn't have the opportunity,' she snapped. Why was he so...*smug*?

'Don't look daggers at me,' Alessandro remarked mildly. 'I'm only teasing.'

A remark that put Liane into a complete tizzy, because she had no idea how to take it. Was he teasing? Or was he just being contrary? Or maybe she was? She shook her head, her gaze on the floor as they continued to dance.

'You're really quite something,' Alessandro remarked as he whirled her around a final time, the music coming to a finish with a swell of the orchestra. 'I can't decide if you're a mouse or a virago.'

'Oh, a mouse, most certainly,' Liane managed, stung by his verdict. In truth she didn't know which was the worse one to be. 'And look, here is Ella, waiting for you. How perfect.'

She turned away, not trusting the look on her face as she walked quickly from the dance floor.

'Liane—' Ella began, and she shook her head.

'Please, go and dance.' She didn't wait to see if Ella did as she'd bid. She didn't want to look.

The rest of the evening passed interminably. Alessandro danced with Ella again, and then stayed by her side as they laughed and chatted, moving through the various groups mingling in the ballroom. Liane made sure never to be near them; she didn't want to be the butt of one of Alessandro's remarks again.

Would Ella fall in love with Alessandro? she wondered. Ella, she knew, loved to fall in love, something Liane had never been able to understand.

'Don't worry, my heart can't actually be broken,' Ella had told her more than once. 'It's made of rubber—it practically bounces! I *like* falling in love, Liane. It's the best feeling in the world, like tumbling through stars! You should try it.'

Liane always smiled and said nothing because she had no intention of doing something so reckless, so dangerous. A heart was a very precious thing and she guarded hers closely, waiting for the right moment. The right man, if he even existed. She hoped he did, but on her bad days she wondered.

She was twenty-seven years old and she'd only gone on a handful of dates, none of them leading anywhere. She hadn't yet found anyone who would make her want more, or dare for the daydream she cast for herself in lonely moments—a hazy world of children and dogs, love and laughter, ease and comfort. The kind of home she'd once had and lost, with the death of her father so many years ago. The kind of life she longed for but was afraid to try to find.

Liane glanced again at Alessandro and Ella. They were standing very close together in the centre of the ballroom. He was murmuring in her ear and she was smiling in that teasing, catlike way that Liane knew she practised in the mirror. She'd seen her do it. Her stomach cramped and she turned away. She was happy for her sister, very happy, of course, but that didn't mean she had to take a front row seat to the unfolding of her fairy tale romance.

A balmy breeze blew in from the penthouse's terrace and Liane moved through the crowd to step outside, enjoying the sultry air on her face. The terrace ran along all four sides of the impressive ballroom, affording a panoramic view of the city. Liane moved away from a few chatting couples, hardly needing the reminder of her own single status.

She'd never minded so much before; she was generally happy with her job, happy with herself. Content, at least. *Mostly*, even if she liked to daydream.

As she gazed out at the city she found herself thinking about Alessandro. The mocking gleam in his eyes, the way his mobile mouth had quirked. He was infuriating and annoying and yet even when she'd been angry she'd felt *alive* in his arms. She could remember exactly how humour had flashed in his eyes, turning them to silver, and how, strangely, the way he'd looked at her had made her feel *seen*, in a way she hadn't before...

The distant chiming of a clock somewhere in the city had Liane giving herself a mental shake. Was it

midnight already? Time to go home, then. She'd find
Ella first, and—

She drew her breath in sharply as she caught sight
of a familiar slender figure on the pavement far below,
dressed in gauzy silk and diamantes, her dress flowing out behind her in a silken stream as she ran down
the front steps of the hotel. *Ella.* Why was she leaving
the ball in such a rush? Liane's stomach cramped with
anxiety. What had happened?

She whirled away from the terrace, stumbling
through the doors to get back into the ballroom and
downstairs to find her sister. She had to push her way
through the milling crowds, catching snatches of gossip as she headed towards the bank of elevators.

'Who is she? Whoever she is, she's clearly captured
his interest—'

'The Prince of Manhattan's found his Princess,
then? He's always seemed so remote—'

'But she just disappeared. Ran out like the building was on fire—'

Finally Liane reached the elevator and stabbed the
button to go down. She scrabbled for her phone in her
handbag, but when she dialled Ella's number there was
no answer. Her sister was awful about answering her
phone, which was somewhat absurd considering how
glued she was to social media.

'Phones aren't for *calling* people,' she'd told Liane
once, as if stating something patently obvious.

The elevator doors finally opened and Liane hurried
in, counting down all twenty-four floors to the mag-
nificent lobby, all marble and crystal and gilt. It was

empty now, for everyone was still up at the ball, but as she came outside onto the steps she stopped suddenly, her breath coming out in a rush, for while her sister might have disappeared, Alessandro Rossi, looking as devastating as ever, was standing right in front of her.

'You again.'

Alessandro Rossi narrowed his eyes in speculation as he surveyed Ella's stepsister, who had stopped abruptly in front of him, her chest heaving. He realised he was enjoying the sight, more than a bit. Her hair had tumbled from its pins and lay over her shoulders in disordered silvery-gold waves. Her cheeks were flushed, her eyes sparkling—not so colourless after all, then. Right now she looked vibrant and alive, like a tiny, perfect jewel.

'Where's Ella?' she demanded breathlessly.

'I have no idea.' He lifted the glass shoe he'd found lying on the step, like some sort of art installation or perhaps a weapon, glittering under the streetlights. 'She left this, though.'

Liane stared at the high-heeled shoe with a flash of recognition, as if she'd seen it before. 'She *left* it?'

'So it would seem. It was lying rather artfully on the steps as I came out. Just the one, of course, like the fairy tale.' A deliberate ploy? But what on earth for?

Liane pressed her lips together and then gave a short nod of acceptance, perhaps understanding. Alessandro's eyes narrowed further. He'd sensed the connection between Ella and her stepsister; Ella had spoken about her with careless affection, while Liane seemed to have appointed herself as Ella's minder. 'Do you know what this is about?' he asked, his tone turning terse.

'What do you mean?'

'I get the feeling something is going on. Something has been planned.' And if there was one thing he hated it was being used for someone else's purposes. He would not be that boy trotted out into the living room years ago, obediently hugging his mother and father while everyone watched and his parents pretended. No, never again.

'Nothing has been planned,' Liane said, but she sounded cautious. Uncertain.

Alessandro didn't know how or why, but something about this whole bizarre scenario felt like a set-up. Why had Ella run off like that, without so much as a word? She'd made such a scene, sprinting through the ballroom, her hair and dress both flying out behind her. Rather fetching, really, if a bit clichéd and overdone. *A bit staged.* What was really going on? 'Do you know where Ella went?' he asked.

'No.' She pressed her lips together and again Alessandro felt there was something she wasn't saying. Something about this whole situation definitely felt off, and he intended to find out what it was. He was not about to be played, not by Ella, not by her mousy stepsister. Not by anyone.

'Are you sure?' She nodded, and he gave her a measured look. Was he being fanciful in seeing something vulnerable and strangely touching in the determined tilt of her chin? In any case, he needed to get to the bottom of this absurd little drama—and quash it. 'Why don't we conduct this conversation somewhere a bit more private?' he suggested, his tone as cool as hers.

Something sparked in her eyes, although the look she gave him was guarded. 'And where would that be?'

'I have a private suite in the hotel.'

A huff of maidenly suspicion escaped her in a gust as her body straightened, practically twanging with indignation. 'Your private suite!' The words were full of outraged incredulity, almost making him smile. She sounded like a scandalised spinster.

'It is fully staffed, and has a study,' he assured her, 'but if you're worried for your virtue, as far as I'm concerned the hotel bar will do just as well, trust me.'

Colour flared more deeply in her face. 'I'm not sure what more I can tell you,' she answered stiffly, 'but as I am concerned for my sister, I would certainly like to hear your account of the evening.'

So she would take him to task! Again he had the urge to smile; he found, bizarrely, he was enjoying her display of spirit. Virago more than mouse, then. 'Very well,' he said, and gave a little courtly bow. 'After you.'

With her head held high—and even then only reaching a bit past his shoulder—she marched past him, back into the hotel, while Alessandro followed, pocketing the shoe.

The hotel bar was a comfortable bastion of leather and mahogany, tucked in the back of the lobby, the only person in sight the weary bartender polishing glasses behind the bar. He snapped to attention when Alessandro stalked into the space, lifting two fingers and pointing to a bottle of whisky glinting in the cabinet behind him before guiding the woman to a discreet nook in the back.

'I realise,' he said as he sat down and the woman perched stiffly opposite him, her back ramrod-straight, 'that I don't actually know your full name.'

'Liane Blanchard.'

'You're French?' She nodded. So he'd been right about that accent. For some reason this pleased him. 'What are you doing in New York?'

'I thought you wished to discuss my sister.'

'It's all relevant, I assure you.'

'Is it?' Again with that chin-tilt, the flash of violet in her eyes. She might have been pale and small but she still had fire, even if he wondered whether she re-alised she did. 'Perhaps I should be the one asking the questions.'

'Oh, do you think so? And why is that?'

'Because my sister ran off into the night, clearly distressed—'

'On the contrary, she wasn't distressed at all.' Alessandro cut her off, his tone turning cool as he recalled Ella's bizarre antics. 'We were having a discussion and she suddenly took off, without a moment's notice.'

Liane cocked her head, scepticism evident in her eyes. 'Just like that?'

'As a matter of fact, yes. Just like that. And left this shoe.' With mocking deliberation he placed the shoe on the table between them. 'Now that is what I call a ridiculous shoe.'

A smile burst across her face like sunlight and then disappeared. He found he was grinning back just for a second, everything in him lightening despite his instinctive suspicion. 'All of Ella's shoes are ridiculous,' she conceded, 'but these more than most, it's true.'

He didn't miss the deep affection in her voice; clearly the sisters were close, and yet so very different. Ella had been bubbly and gregarious, laughing and light and easy to talk to, if a bit, well, *insipid*. He'd been bored, but not as bored as he usually was, and the paparazzi had almost certainly taken the publicity shots they'd needed. He'd been ready to call it a night before Ella had decided to, by sprinting out of the ballroom.

And meanwhile Liane was quiet and contained, yet with those beguiling flashes of fire, those incredible eyes…still waters ran deep, and Alessandro supposed hers ran very deep indeed.

The bartender appeared with the bottle of whisky and two glasses and Alessandro tossed the shoe onto a chair to make way for their drinks.

'I don't drink whisky,' Liane informed him coolly after the bartender had left.

Unperturbed, Alessandro poured a finger of whisky in each glass. 'There's always a first time.'

She folded her arms and attempted to stare him down. 'You're rather…controlling, aren't you?'

'I prefer to think of it as being hospitable.' He proffered her the glass, and after a second's pause she took it. 'But by all means don't drink if you don't want to. It seemed rude not to offer you a whisky when I'm having one myself.' And with that he took one long, burning swallow, grateful for the heat hitting the back of his throat.

Liane put her glass down without giving it so much as a sniff. 'I'm worried about my sister,' she stated almost defiantly.

'I told you,' he replied calmly, 'she was in no way distressed. At all.'

'I know what you said, and in truth I'm inclined to believe you.' She paused, pursing her lips, a little wrinkle appearing in the creamy smoothness of her forehead. 'But she can be quite—impetuous sometimes about things. And to leave the ball that way...' She let out a soft gasp of realisation, biting the soft fullness of her lower lip, and Alessandro's gaze narrowed. 'Of *course*,' she whispered, and then she let out a little laugh, a sound that reminded Alessandro, bizarrely, of the bubbles in champagne. He wanted to hear it again, even as he recognised he'd been right. Something *had* been going on, and Liane knew what it was.

'What?' he demanded. 'What do you know? What's so funny?'

'It's not funny really, but it's classic Ella.' She sighed as she leaned back against the leather cushions of her seat, her body relaxing so for once she didn't look so uptight, so anxious. 'Ella might have told you; she's something of a social media influencer, although she's just getting started. The glass shoes were given to her by some up-and-coming designer—she must have left one on purpose. The clock strikes midnight, Cinderella at the ball, et cetera.' She sighed, shaking her head. 'And she's gone off wearing one shoe, and is now probably going to vlog the whole thing as some modern take on the fairy tale.'

He frowned, feeling not much more the wiser. 'Vlog?'

She wrinkled her nose, letting out another one of those tinkly little laughs. 'A video blog. I'm a social media dinosaur, but even I know what a vlog is, although I suppose that's because of Ella.'

'So this is nothing more than a publicity stunt,' he surmised slowly, hating the thought, and Liane nodded.

'Yes. Something like that. At least I think so. That would be Ella's style.'

He wasn't surprised, based on what he already knew of Ella, and yet he still felt distrustful. Irritated too, because he did not want to be used in her little ploys and games. And yet, he told himself with the cold logic he prided himself on, he'd basically been using Ella for publicity, making sure they were snapped together to promote the hotel and make it seem so *fun*. If all the while she'd been using him, well, there was a fitting sort of rightness to it, or there could be, even if it went against every instinct he'd ever had. He never allowed himself to be used, not since he'd been a helpless child.

No, if anything, he was the one who would do the using and, considering all he had learned, Ella Ash would suit his purposes admirably. Their association would not end here, for both of their benefits. And if this intriguing woman came as part of the bargain…

'Very good,' he told Liane, and tossed back the rest of his whisky, levelling his iron gaze on her own startled one. 'Then you can help me find her.'

CHAPTER THREE

'ALESSANDRO ROSSI WANTS to see me?'

Ella's eyebrows rose in two golden arcs as she lounged back on the sofa in her pyjamas. A small knowing smile curved her mouth. 'Must have been the shoes.'

'It must have,' Liane agreed, 'or the gorgeous dress or your stunning looks or your sparkling personality. Perhaps all three—or four, even.'

Ella laughed, tossing her head back against the pillows. 'Stop it, I'm blushing.'

Not as much as she'd been blushing last night, when she'd been sitting alone in that bar with Alessandro, remembering how he'd looked down at her with such amusement. *I can't decide if you're a mouse or a virago.* Well, she'd been a virago last night, stung into tart replies by his own self-assured arrogance. This wasn't about her, Liane reminded herself. It was, as ever, about Ella.

'He wants to meet you at his office this afternoon,' she told her stepsister, 'so you ought to get dressed.'

'But it's Saturday.' Ella's eyes fluttered closed as

she let out a deep, breathy sigh. 'And I'm exhausted. I was out till five in the morning, you know. Alonso was having a party in Soho—'

'I guess you didn't turn into a pumpkin, then.'

'It's the *carriage* that turns into a pumpkin, Liane. Get your fairy tales straight.' She laughed as she opened her eyes. 'Wasn't that an amazing stunt, though? I put the video up at two o'clock this morning and it already has *fifty thousand* hits.' A bubble of delighted, incredulous laughter escaped her as she reached for her phone and started scrolling. 'Sixty thousand now! Liane, I'm practically viral.'

'Amazing that the term is a compliment.'

'You know what I mean.'

'Yes, I do. What video was this?'

'Of Alessandro finding the shoe, of course.' Ella leaned back against the sofa, a smug smile curving her lips.

'You filmed him?' Liane asked, uneasy at the thought.

'Of course.'

Judging from what little she knew of the man, Liane doubted he would be pleased. He'd certainly acted suspicious last night, demanding to know why Ella had left—and not out of concern either. He seemed, she thought, a quiet, controlled sort of person, someone who prized restraint over emotion. Someone utterly unlike Ella. She sighed and glanced at her watch. It was already past noon, and last night Alessandro Rossi had asked—demanded, really—that Ella appear at his office in midtown at two o'clock sharp. Liane's first instinct had been to refuse on principle; Alessandro Rossi alarmed her as much as he fascinated her, and she wasn't entirely sure what he wanted with her stepsister. Then she realised how beneficial a meeting with him could be for Ella's career aspirations, such as they were. Not that she knew much about social media influencing herself, but still.

Even though he'd only arrived a few months ago, Alessandro Rossi was already one of the most famous men in the city—handsome, wealthy, powerful, reclusive and thought to be of Italian nobility. Finding out what he wanted with Ella would surely be the savvy thing to do. *And it has nothing to do with you wanting to see him again.*

'Don't you want to start getting ready?' Liane cajoled. 'This could be your big break, Ella.'

She stretched one foot, studying the silver nail polish on her toes. 'What do you think he wants?'

'I have no idea.' That wasn't entirely true. When Alessandro had said he wanted to find Ella last night, he'd assured her it was for a business proposition.

'Legitimate,' he'd added sharply when Liane had looked somewhat scandalised. 'I don't have to hire mistresses, Miss Blanchard, if that's what you were thinking. Trust me on that score.'

'I wasn't—' she'd protested rather feebly.

'I can read your expression perfectly. That's not what this is about. At all.' Which had reassured her to a rather ridiculous degree, even as she'd told herself not to be a fool. Alessandro would never think of her that way. It wouldn't even occur to him.

'Then what is it about?' she'd asked, doing her best not to blush as she imagined what Alessandro Rossi's *mistresses* might be like.

'A business opportunity that will advantage your sister's interests as well as my own. Now, please get her to my office at two o'clock sharp tomorrow if she wants to know the details.' And he'd handed her his business card by way of dismissal.

'No idea at all?' Ella pressed, lifting her head to regard Liane from her lazy sprawl on the sofa. 'What did he say to you?'

'He did mention some sort of business proposition,' Liane allowed, 'but I have no idea what it could be. Still, I imagine it might be worth listening to, at least.' Normally Liane would have advised caution—a word her sister did not take too much to heart—but she was honest enough to acknowledge that she was, somewhat guardedly, encouraging her sister to attend this meeting not just because of the opportunity it could provide but because she wanted to see Alessandro Rossi again. She wasn't sure whether she trusted or even liked him, but when she was in his presence she felt... electrified. More alive than she'd ever felt before, as if every nerve and sense had sprung to quivering life. Which of course was ridiculous, and yet...

True.

'So?' she prompted, nudging Ella's foot. 'Are you going to go?'

'Oh, I suppose.' Ella yawned hugely. 'I mean, for curiosity's sake more than anything else.'

'What did you talk about with him last night?' Liane asked.

'I don't really remember. Basic chitchat. Dull stuff, mostly. He can be charming, but it felt a bit like an act. Almost like he didn't really want to be there.'

'He's known to be somewhat reclusive.' According to the tabloids, anyway. Alessandro Rossi did not socialise or appear in public except for work, something that had made him an enigma, and an attractive one at that.

'In other words, boring.' Ella yawned again, her eyes fluttering closed, and Liane couldn't believe her sister was going to let this opportunity slip through her fingers. Typical Ella—ambitious only when she felt like it.

'*Ella.*' She nudged her foot again. 'If you're going to go you should have started getting ready ten minutes ago.'

Ella cracked open an eye to gaze at her speculatively. 'Why are you so determined to get me there?'

Don't blush. 'It's a good opportunity for you. Or at least it might be.'

'I suppose.' Ella let out another enormous yawn as she stretched languorously and then finally, in a tangle of golden limbs, rose from the sofa. 'Oh, all right, okay, I'll go, if just to satisfy your curiosity.'

'I'm not—' Liane began, but Ella just laughed all the way upstairs.

At two minutes to two o'clock they were standing in front of an imposing skyscraper that looked to be made almost entirely of opaque black glass that soared up to the summery blue sky, a beacon of dark modernity in the middle of the city.

'Wow.' Ella lowered her sunglasses to survey the building with appreciation. 'He owns the whole building?'

Liane nodded at the discreet gold plaque to the side of the door on which was written 'Rossi Enterprises'. 'It appears so, or at least his family does.' She'd done an Internet search on Alessandro Rossi that morning, forcing herself away from all the articles of spurious speculation in the online tabloids and on gossip sites, heading for a simple encyclopaedia entry that told her Alessandro was the only son of Leonardo Rossi; his father had handed the business to him last year and retired to Ibiza; there was no mention of his mother. He was notoriously reclusive, with very little known about his private life, and Rossi Enterprises was worth billions.

'Well, then, maybe this is worth satisfying your curiosity,' Ella proclaimed and with a glinting smile for Liane she sashayed inside the office building and promptly charmed the grim-faced, black-suited man at the door, who told her Mr Rossi was expecting her.

Liane's stomach tightened with nerves as they soared upwards towards Alessandro Rossi's penthouse office. She wasn't nervous about seeing him again, not precisely, more about him seeing how she reacted to him. This silly schoolgirl infatuation she had stupidly developed over a stranger needed to stop—especially if it showed on her face. She couldn't bear to be revealed in such a way, and she had a sense that Alessandro would be able to guess exactly what she was thinking—and feeling—which was a rather horrifying thought.

Why did she have to react to the man this way? If anything, his high-handed manner should annoy her and nothing more. Yet even now her body was tingling with anticipation, excitement fizzing through her veins, simply at the prospect of seeing him again.

A solemn-looking assistant in a sleek dark suit met them at the elevator and escorted them to an imposing pair of wood-panelled doors. Liane could feel her heart thumping as Ella went in first, head held high, looking as fabulous as she always did in a tastefully clinging yellow sheath and matching open-toed heels, her hair in glossy golden waves about her shoulders. Liane slipped in behind, staying near the wall as Ella strode towards Alessandro's desk.

'I heard you had a proposition for me,' she said, *almost* making it sound dirty.

Alessandro rose from behind his desk in one fluid movement, his face expressionless, his powerful body encased in an expertly tailored charcoal-grey suit that brought out the silver in his eyes. He looked powerful and remote and completely in control and, stupidly, Liane's heart fluttered. She really needed to get to grips with these absurd feelings of hers. Fortunately—or not—and just as she'd expected, he wasn't even looking at her.

'Miss Ash. So glad you could meet me. Please, sit.' He gestured to one of the leather club chairs in front of his massive desk, the floor-to-ceiling windows giving a panoramic view of the city, glinting skyscrapers all around, Central Park a haze of green in the distance. His gaze flicked once, very briefly, to Liane, revealing nothing, yet even so Liane felt as if she'd been jolted with electricity, a second's blazing connection—at least for her. 'And you, Miss Blanchard, as well, of course,' he added smoothly. Was there a hint of humour in his voice? Liane wasn't sure, but she blushed anyway.

'Thank you,' she murmured as she came forward. She perched on the edge of her chair as he stood behind his desk, surveying them both, before he reached down to retrieve something.

'I believe this belongs to you,' he told Ella, bringing out the silly glass shoe with a mocking flourish.

Ella, always rising to the occasion, laughed and raised one slender leg. 'You should see if it fits first,' she told him with a deliberate flutter of her eyelashes.

'Very well,' he said, his face expressionless. His gaze flicked, ever so briefly, to Liane, before he removed her sister's sandal and, without any innuendo or enthusiasm, slid the glass shoe on her foot.

'A perfect fit,' he remarked dryly as he stood back.

Ella's eyes danced. 'So this is when you ask me to marry you, right? And we live happily ever after.' She tossed her head back, giving a throaty laugh. 'Somehow I don't think that was the business proposition you intended to put to me.' She flipped off the glass shoe and replaced her sandal as she gave him a forthright look, the glass slipper dangling from one manicured finger. 'So, Mr Rossi, what exactly is this business proposition?'

* * *

Ella Ash was a firecracker, that much was obvious. Alessandro kept his gaze even and expressionless as he fought both amusement and annoyance at her blatant theatrics. His suspicions from last night were clearly confirmed today; she was the type of person who was constantly performing, needing an invisible audience everywhere she went. A lot like his mother had been, and exactly the kind of exhibitionism he hated, and yet in this case she might be just what he needed, at least for a brief time. For the sake of Rossi Hotels.

His gaze flickered once more to Liane. He found he couldn't stop looking at her, trying to gauge what emotion seethed behind those opaque violet eyes, her mouth pursed, her hands in her lap. She wore a plain blue shirtdress, a rather matronly outfit, and yet he was still conscious of her lithe curves, the way the belt at her waist emphasised its slenderness. She was perfectly petite, delicate in every way, and he found her far more fascinating than the obvious Ella. Gold compared to gilt, he reflected, before banishing the thought.

He turned back to Ella. 'My business proposition is simple. Rossi Hotels is in need of a younger ambassador. Our brand of unparalleled luxury, comfort and privacy has not been translating as well to the social media generation.' He quirked his mouth wryly, inviting Ella into the joke, if there even was one. He hated the whole concept of courting publicity, but he hated failure even more.

He'd spent the last ten years building Rossi Enterprises back up from the ashes after his father had so carelessly let it burn near to the ground, and he'd be damned if he let any part of it smoulder away now, simply because the millennial generation needed to see something on Instagram before they paid money. At least with this he could control the attention, the narrative.

'Is that right?' Ella cocked her head. 'I will say, the hotel did seem a little stuffy to me.'

He forced a small, tight smile of acknowledgement. 'So, as I'm sure you've been able to guess, this is where you come in.'

'Do you want me to feature the hotel on my vlog?' Her eyes widened. 'Because the video of you finding the glass shoe has got...' she paused to reach for her phone, scrolling with lightning speed '...two hundred thousand views! Can you believe it?'

'What?' His voice sharpened as he stared at her hard. 'What video?'

'You mean you asked me here without even seeing it?' she exclaimed with a peal of delighted laughter. 'Look.'

She handed him her phone and, frowning, Alessandro gazed down at a somewhat blurry video of, he saw, himself, walking down the steps of his hotel. The camera zoomed in on the glass slipper, lying so artfully on the ground, and then on his face as he picked it up, turned it over in his hands. She'd put text over the last image—*OMG, the Prince found my slipper!! What next??*—which made Alessandro suppress a wince. Seriously, this stuff was both excruciating and infantile, and yet it seemed to work, because in the few seconds it had taken for him to view the damned thing the video had garnered a thousand more views. Insane. And not in a good way. He had a whole churning mess of feelings about being secretly filmed and viewed, being trotted out and *used*, and none of them were good.

Right then and there he fought the deep-seated instinct to fling the phone on the floor, ground it to crushed glass beneath his heel and show Ella Ash the door. *How dared she use him?* He, who would never let himself be used.

And yet, pushing down those heated emotions, he forced himself not to react. He'd suspected she'd been using him last night; now his suspicions had been confirmed. It didn't change his own purpose.

No, he would choose for it not to. Choose control and restraint over anger and emotion, as he always did. Choose to be unlike either of his parents, led by emotion and desire, careering into desperation and misery and using him in the process. Silently he handed the phone back and Ella pocketed it. Liane, he saw out of the corner of his eye, hadn't said a word, although she was definitely looking apprehensive, her violet gaze darting between him and her sister, golden lashes sweeping down when she caught him looking at her.

'So,' he surmised in a clipped voice, 'you took that video of me from some hiding place, I presume?'

'An Uber in the street.' Ella was flippantly unrepentant. Was this sort of behaviour normal among this generation? Alessandro wondered. At thirty-four he was only twelve years older than Ella, but right now he felt utterly ancient.

'And posted it without my knowledge or consent?' he pressed, his voice hardening.

Ella's eyes widened. 'Is that even a thing?'

It was debatable, Alessandro supposed, considering he'd been in a public place, but he was not going to argue the legalities of taking and posting footage of another person right now. 'Just what was the purpose of your little glass slipper stunt, may I ask?'

'My friend Alonso Alovar made the shoes. It was meant to be some publicity for him and, trust me, it's working, because his website has already crashed from all the orders.'

'How did they know they were his shoes?'

'From the hashtags.' She shook her head slowly, her eyes dancing with amusement. 'Do you even know how social media works?'

No, and he didn't really have any desire to know, had never needed to know. Oh, he understood that things went viral, and people got pathetically famous for fifteen minutes through some absurd post or other, yes, *fine*, but it didn't affect real life. His life. The world of business and banking, investments and enterprise, stocks and bonds and cold, hard cash. Except perhaps now it might. Unfortunately.

'I've never had a need or interest in using social media,' he told her levelly, 'but, as I stated before, I am interested in engaging with the medium for the purposes of publicity for the hotels.'

'Don't put that in a tweet,' Ella quipped, and he shook his head in exasperation.

'This is what I propose—for you to join me on a

brief tour of the Rossi hotels that I have been planning. It's our centenary this year, and there will be parties hosted at each hotel to celebrate the anniversary throughout the next week. In fact, there is one in Los Angeles tomorrow night.' He'd only been intending to make a brief appearance at a few of the events, but that would have to change now. He'd have to go to every one and stay for at least an hour, chatting and mingling, with Ella at his side. How interminable.

'A tour?' Ella's eyes rounded, her lips parting. 'You want me to go on a tour with you?'

'Yes, the idea is we would go together and it would be covered publicly by the magazines, et cetera.'

'Together?' Ella asked, her eyes dancing. 'I mean, *together* together?'

She was teasing him, but Alessandro decided to take her seriously. Best to be clear about what he wanted—and what he definitely didn't. For a second he had an urge to look at Liane again, but he resisted it. 'Together for the purposes of publicity only, I assure you. As charming as you may be, Miss Ash, this really is a business proposition and nothing more.'

'And then I post about it all on social media?' she surmised, her voice rising in excitement. 'A whole series—like a story, one post per day? We could follow on from the glass slipper—Prince Charming finds his Princess! What happens next? Where do they go? It would be *brilliant*.'

'I had not considered such an angle,' Alessandro replied, 'but it might be effective.' It sounded like an awful, cheap gimmick to him, but it seemed this was what the world had come to. 'The main thing is that you highlight the hotels, not some ridiculous story.' He glanced at Liane, who was looking rather severe. 'Do you disapprove?' he asked and, startled, she jumped a little, her gaze skating away from his.

'Why should I disapprove?'

He didn't know exactly, but he still sensed that she did. There was something distasteful about the whole thing, even *especially* to him. He didn't court publicity. He hated attention. This was not the way he operated at all, and yet here he was. For the sake of the hotels. For the sake of Rossi Enterprises. And this time he would be in control.

There's no other reason you're doing it, is there?

He banished that sly internal voice as he gave a dismissive shrug. 'You tell me.'

Liane didn't meet his eyes as she answered. 'I don't disapprove, Mr Rossi, although it's not for me to disapprove or approve. This is Ella's decision.'

'Indeed.' He turned back to Ella. 'There are two Rossi hotels in America—one in Los Angeles and the one here in New York, and three in Europe—London, Paris and Rome. The parties are planned over the next week.' Which was a fair amount of time to be gallivanting around the world with Ella Ash in tow, but he could work remotely and it would also provide him with the opportunity to check in on each hotel, which he'd been planning to do over the next few months anyway. All in all, a worthwhile exercise, or so he hoped. 'I'll remunerate you for your time, of course, and provide you with accommodation and travel, as well as the necessary wardrobe accoutrements.'

'I can provide the wardrobe,' Ella assured him. 'This will be an amazing opportunity for some of the designers I work with. Trust me, you won't be disappointed.'

He gave a brief nod of acceptance. 'Very well. All I ask is that I see and sign off on every message or photo before you post it.' He might not be social media savvy, but he knew well enough how things could spiral out of control online and he had no intention of being made a fool of. Ever. Already he feared this project was ill-advised. At least it was only a week.

Ella cocked her head, pursing her lips. 'Agreed, but you've got to trust me. Judging from what I've seen so far, what you think works on social media might actually not.'

He inclined his head in terse acknowledgement. 'Naturally I'm willing to take advice on the matter, but I will have the ultimate say.' Of that he would not be dissuaded.

'Okay.' She smiled at him, a dazzling display of teeth and eyes, all sparkle and shine, making him wonder just how much there actually was underneath.

'So you agree?' he asked, raising his eyebrows.

'Yes, but I have one condition.'

'Oh?' His tone cooled. 'And what is that?'

'Liane comes with me.'

Liane made some small, startled noise, her hand flying to her mouth. Alessandro glanced at her, noticing the way her eyes widened above her hand, as soft and purple as a bed of pansies; clearly she was as surprised as he was by this suggestion. 'I am not opposed,' he stated, realising with a slight jolt just how much he meant it.

'Good, because I need Liane.'

He raised his eyebrows. 'Need her?'

'For moral support and companionship.' Ella's tone was staunch. 'She comes or I don't.'

'No need for ultimatums.' He was not, he realised, opposed to the idea at all. Quite the contrary. He glanced at Liane, who was still looking rather shocked, a blush turning her cheeks a delicate pink. 'Are you able to take time off work?' He realised he didn't even know if she worked, or what she did with her time, her life; he basically knew nothing about her at all.

Slowly she removed her hand from her mouth, still looking shaken. 'I'm a teacher and we broke for summer vacation last week, so, yes…in theory.'

'In theory? You are willing to accompany us?'

Liane glanced at Ella. 'You don't really need me, do you, Ella?' she asked quietly.

'I do,' Ella insisted. 'You're sensible and no-nonsense and I'll fall to pieces without you. You know I will. I always do.' She reached for Liane's hands, squeezing them in her own. 'Please, Liane. I need you. Truly.'

Liane glanced uncertainly between Ella and Alessandro, clearly torn. Why was she so reluctant? he wondered with a pinch of irritation. At least he thought that was what it was. He was offering an all-expenses-paid trip to some of the world's top destinations, while staying at a series of luxury hotels. She should be thanking her lucky stars or, really, *him*.

'Well?' he asked, a touch of impatience in his voice.

Liane took a deep breath, and then she nodded as she squeezed Ella's hands before releasing them. 'All right,' she said, her tone making it sound as if she were agreeing to something frightening or dangerous rather than a luxury vacation. 'I'll do it. I'll go.'

CHAPTER FOUR

SHE REALLY NEEDED to pinch herself. Liane glanced out of the window of the private jet at the cerulean sky, a few fleecy clouds scudding by. In a little over an hour they were going to be landing in Los Angeles. How crazy was that? Forty-eight hours ago Alessandro Rossi had stepped on her toes. Now she was in his private plane, about to jet around the world. Not that he'd looked at her once since taking off. Or even Ella, for that matter. It was as if, once this bizarre deal had been agreed, they'd both more or less ceased to exist.

She glanced at Ella, who was sprawled in the wide leather seat across from her, fingers flying over her phone as usual. Liane almost wished she was interested in social media the way Ella was, anything to distract her from her own circling thoughts, the uneasy, anxious restlessness coursing through her.

Why had Ella insisted she come along on this crazy trip? And why had she agreed? Of course she knew the answers to both questions—Ella had always counted on her common sense, and she'd agreed because she never said no to her sister.

And because you wanted to spend more time with Alessandro Rossi.

Even if he wasn't looking at her. Even if he almost certainly hadn't thought about her once since suggesting this plan.

Unable to keep herself from it, Liane glanced at the seat diagonally from hers, where Alessandro was poring over some papers on the table in front of him, dark, straight brows drawn together over those hooded eyes. His lashes fanned his cheeks as he read—thick, dark velvety lashes that still somehow made him look masculine. Strange, that. He shifted in his seat, recrossing his legs, and Liane breathed in the citrusy tang of his aftershave.

She turned back to the window, determined to focus on the blue sky and not the man across from her, whose very presence made her senses swim. A party tonight in Los Angeles, and another in London two days after that—it made her head spin. Her mother had been stunned by the sudden turn of events, but also unbearably, pragmatically hopeful.

'This is your chance to make a good match, Liane!' she'd exclaimed. 'Finally, you can find yourself a husband. Do not waste this opportunity. Make the most of yourself, if you can.'

'Alessandro Rossi doesn't have eyes for me, Maman,' Liane had told her, trying to sound rueful rather than forlorn.

'Not Rossi, of course,' Amelie dismissed. 'He's above your league, to be sure.' Liane did her best not to look stung; she knew her mother was only speaking the truth in her usual blunt way. Alessandro Rossi was way, way above her league. 'But someone else, perhaps?' Amelie suggested. 'Someone who works for him, an assistant or acquaintance? You are bound to meet many eligible men in your travels. You must keep your eye out, and make sure to look your best. I will pack the blue gown.'

Circa nineteen eighty-three, Liane had thought with a shudder. Her mother was well-intentioned if decidedly misguided. 'And what if I don't want to get married?' she'd asked, half teasing. 'What if I don't want to hook a man like a fish?' Not that she even could. She wouldn't even know how to try. She'd always hoped one day a man might sweep into her life, and her into his arms. She wouldn't have to go looking for love because it would find her, bowl her over.

'Bah.' Her mother waved her hand in dismissal. 'What else would you do with a man?'

The memory made Liane both sigh and smile now. Despite her mother's near-constant criticism, she felt sorry for her, soured by two expedient marriages that hadn't turned out to be so expedient after all. Her own father had been a lovable gambler, and Robert Ash had been extravagant in his largesse and hopeless with money. Amelie had been left nearly destitute—twice. No wonder she had become both bitter and pragmatic, taking out her disappointments on her daughters. Manon had learned not to care, but Liane still had to work not to let it hurt.

She wasn't sure whether her mother had been deeply in love with either of her husbands, but she suspected she'd at least felt some affection for them. Not the fairy tale, though, she thought with a sigh. Perhaps such epic love stories, glass slippers included, were really only for fiction. She certainly hadn't seen any evidence for them, just the manufactured appearance of them on social media, and yet still, she knew, she secretly yearned for it to happen to her one day. Not the glass slipper, but the Prince. The sweet and sure certainty of finding a man who understood her, who loved her, who *saw* her truly. She didn't necessarily believe there was only one man out there for her, but she hoped there was at least one. Somewhere. Some day…but not, she reminded herself, today.

'How many views now?' she asked her sister, and Ella looked up from her phone.

'Six hundred thousand. It's insane.' She glanced at Alessandro, her eyes full of humour. 'How come you're so famous?'

'Because my family is one of Italy's oldest noble lines and has been foremost in European investments for one hundred years,' he replied without looking up from the papers he was reading.

'And yet you need me.' Ella's voice was full of laughing flirtatiousness.

Alessandro looked up then, one eyebrow quirked. 'Consider this more of a social experiment than anything born of true necessity, Miss Ash. The Rossi hotels are merely one branch of the business as a whole.' He shrugged, returning his gaze to his papers. 'My fortune is hardly dependent upon them, but naturally I wish them to succeed, and if engagement with social media is necessary...' A pause as he made a tick on one of the papers. 'Then so be it.'

'Oh, and here I thought I was saving the day,' Ella teased.

Alessandro gave her a level look before one corner of his mouth reluctantly kicked up, making Liane's heart flipflop even though he wasn't looking at her. Ella's smile widened and she batted her eyelashes with her usual laughing drama before turning back to her phone.

Excusing herself with a murmur, Liane rose from her seat. Alessandro had invited them to explore the jet when they'd first boarded, but Liane had been too overawed to do anything but sit down and buckle up. Now she left the main cabin for the ones beyond, curiosity warring with an uneasy restlessness at being here at all.

She certainly didn't need a front row seat to the quips flying between Alessandro and Ella. Alessandro might have said he had no interest in romance, but Liane was quite sure Ella could convince him otherwise if she chose to—and why wouldn't she?

The cabin beyond the main seating area was styled as an office, complete with a wide mahogany desk, the curved walls lined with specially built bookcases. Liane trailed her finger along the titles—classics of philosophy, poetry and history in a variety of languages. She wondered if Alessandro had read them all or if they were just for show. She selected a volume of poetry and let the book fall open naturally to a well-worn marked page—*Demain, dès l'aube*, by Victor Hugo. Slowly she read the familiar lines:

Demain, dès l'aube, à l'heure où blanchit la campagne, Je partirai.

"'Tomorrow at dawn, when the countryside brightens, I will depart.'"

Liane nearly jumped out of her skin as she heard Alessandro huskily quote the poem, his voice seeming to caress every syllable. He'd come into the room without her even realising, close enough to see the page she was reading, and, embarrassed, she realised she was snooping and he knew it.

'You know the poem?' she asked, clumsily closing the book and putting it back on the shelf.

'Very well.' He paused and then continued softly, *"'Vois-tu, je sais que tu m'attends. J'irai par la forêt, j'irai par la montagne.'"*

"'You see,'" Liane translated, her voice as soft as his, *"'I know you will wait for me. I will go through the wood, I will go past the mountains.'"* She shook her head slowly. 'You speak French?'

The smile that quirked his mouth seemed almost tender as his gaze swept over her, leaving a heated, tingling awareness in its wake. *'Mais oui.'*

She laughed a bit unevenly, shocked at how a single look turned her weak at the knees, filled her with a yearning she was afraid to name. He gave a playful grimace of acknowledgement. 'Actually, I only have schoolboy French. I can't speak or write it, really. But it's a beautiful language.' The observation felt strangely intimate, as if he were complimenting her and not her French. When she dared look at him his gaze was pensive, lingering. Something in her trembled and ached.

'Yet you're able to quote Hugo?' she managed as she clasped her hands together in front of her in an attempt to calm her fluttering nerves. 'I'm impressed.'

'I always liked that poem.'

'But it's so sad,' Liane protested, even though she liked it as well. It captured something of the grief she'd felt when her father had embroiled himself in scandal and their lives had changed so drastically—leaving the little house in Lyon, moving to Paris and then to New York, only to have her father die soon after, so they were catapulted into a new life that had felt unfamiliar and even hostile. It was a loss that ran right through her, like silk shot with silver thread, tingeing everything with sorrow, making her stay in the shadows.

'Hugo wrote it for his daughter,' Alessandro remarked, 'who drowned in the Seine when she was newly married.'

Liane nodded, knowing the story. 'Her skirts were too heavy and weighed her down, and her husband died trying to save her. She was only nineteen.'

'Not so much of a fairy tale.'

'But then fairy tales aren't real, are they?' she felt forced to return. She tried to give him a teasing smile but she didn't quite manage it.

He cocked his head, his gaze sweeping slowly over her, making her feel strangely revealed—not as if he were stripping away her clothes but her very soul, plumbing depths that she'd hidden from everyone. Goodness, but she was being fanciful, thinking this man saw something in her that no one else did—of course he didn't. He barely saw her at all. But right now she was in the spotlight of his gaze and it made her burn in ways that were both welcome and uncomfortable. *Oh, to be seen, truly seen...* and yet how utterly terrifying.

'Is that what you think?' he asked.

She was hardly about to admit that she longed to believe in the fairy tale, at least for herself. She wasn't about to spout about true love and the happily-ever-after she yearned for when she already suspected him to be a cynic about such matters, and in any case she didn't have any evidence to substantiate her dreams, just a deep-seated belief, or maybe just hope, that true love did exist somewhere, that it could blossom into something big and wonderful.

'It's what I've seen so far,' she replied as pragmatically as she could. 'Here you are, making up a fairy tale for public consumption.' She'd meant to sound light but her voice came out a bit sharper than she intended.

He arched one eyebrow. 'So you really are disapproving.'

'I'm not disapproving so much as...dubious,' she allowed. 'As to the efficacy or morality of such a scheme.'

'Morality?' He folded his arms so his biceps bulged against the crisp cotton of his shirt, his lush mouth hardened into a frown. 'What is immoral about posting a few images of the Rossi hotels on social media?'

Liane shrugged, discomfited. She wasn't as disapproving, she thought with a pang, as she was jealous, something she would never, ever admit to Alessandro. 'You're bringing Ella along to generate gossip and speculation,' she hedged.

'I'm bringing Ella along,' he corrected, 'to raise the profile of the hotels on social media.'

'But you know she'll make up some silly story through her posts. The Prince and the Princess, et cetera.' She hoped she didn't sound jealous.

Alessandro cocked an eyebrow. 'Will she? I have to sign off on them, remember.' That steely gaze swept over her yet again, creating a wash of awareness in its wake, making everything prickle and heat. 'In any case, you are allowing your sister to take part in it.'

'She's twenty-two,' Liane returned with a hint of acerbity. 'I can't make her decisions for her.'

'Too true.' He propped one shoulder against the bookcase, close enough that Liane could feel the heat of his powerful body, breathe in the citrusy scent of his aftershave that made her senses swim. If she took a step towards him they'd be touching. She imagined the feel of the crisp cotton of his shirt under her hand, the warm skin underneath, even as she strove to stay still and unmoved. Her body, though, felt like swaying towards him, the way a plant might tilt to the sun. So ridiculous. So shaming, especially when she doubted he was feeling anything remotely similar. 'So you'd rather she hadn't agreed?' he pressed. 'That I hadn't suggested such a plan?'

She shook her head, not wanting to be drawn. 'It's not for me to say.'

'But you must have an opinion on the matter,' he observed silkily.

She glanced up at him from beneath her lashes, uneasy to offer an opinion when she—and Ella—were both so dependent on his generosity for the next week. And, she realised, she didn't want him to think her prudish or stern. Schoolmarmish, even, although she knew that was what she was. 'Everyone will think the two of you are falling in love,' she said after a moment, her voice the tiniest bit unsteady.

'They'll wonder,' Alessandro agreed with a shrug. 'What is that to me?'

'Nothing, I suppose.' He obviously didn't care what other people thought about him. 'I suppose I don't like deceiving people,' she stated finally. Although would it really be deception if they did end up falling in love?

'Neither do I,' he replied equably.

She frowned, glancing at him in uneasy confusion. 'But then why...?'

'This is hardly deception,' Alessandro informed her mildly. He angled his body so his shoulder was practically brushing hers, causing every sense to twang to life. She didn't dare move away, and in truth she didn't want to. The citrusy scent of him was making her head spin. 'All marketing is spin, you know. Showing whatever it is in the way you want to. That's all this is.'

Liane nodded slowly. She knew she wasn't actually bothered so much by any seeming element of deception, rather than the simple fact of Alessandro and Ella posing as a couple together. Although he'd implied yesterday that he intended them to be no such thing and even right now seemed to think himself immune to her sister's enviable charms, she still feared it would be inevitable. Ella was gorgeous, charming, funny and always willing to tumble into love. How would a man like Alessandro resist her? He wouldn't, she thought, unable to keep from feeling despondent, even try.

Her eyes, Alessandro thought, were marvellous—the colour of pansies, or perhaps a bruise. A deep, damaged violet, fringed by silvery lashes that swept her pale cheeks every time she blinked, which had been quite a lot. He made her nervous—something that gave him a sense of both remorse and satisfaction. He realised he enjoyed the ability to affect her, to *matter*. It was an alarming thought because normally he didn't want to matter to anyone. Mattering allowed you to hurt and be hurt, to use and be used. He wanted no part of any of that, not even a little bit. Life, he'd long ago determined, needed to be a solitary affair; emotions were not to be engaged.

And yet…he liked the way her eyes widened and her breathing turned uneven when he moved closer to her. He breathed in the flowery scent of her perfume, something subtle and not too sweet. A grown-up fragrance—understated, sophisticated. He felt there was something fragile and vulnerable about her, yet also tensile and strong. A woman of complexities, enigmas, perhaps without her even realising it.

He found her far more fascinating, and even alluring, than her charismatic yet fundamentally insipid sister, who couldn't look up from her phone for more than thirty seconds, and then only to tease or flirt. There were depths to Liane that he hadn't sensed in Ella. But why should he compare the two women? Liane was in her own category altogether.

Not, he reminded himself, that it made a bit of difference to anything. He had no intention of taking this burgeoning attraction between them anywhere, as enjoyable as this moment was, as much as he was now wondering what it would be like to lean forward just a little bit, breathe in her fragrance, slide his fingers along the silkiness of her skin, draw her to him...

'How do you know that poem?' he asked, easing back slightly. He was curious to learn more about her—and direct the conversation away from the social media scheme he was already beginning to regret. It had been a rather recklessly impetuous decision, so unlike him, and if he was honest with himself he feared it had little to do with the state of the Rossi hotels and everything with the woman before him.

'It is taught in school in France. It was one of my favourites. I teach it as well.'

'You grew up in France, then?'

'Yes, in Lyon and then Paris, but we moved to New York when I was eleven.'

'How come?'

'All these questions.' She laughed lightly as she moved away from him with a whisper of fabric over skin, her plain, pale blue cotton sundress swishing about her slender legs. 'My father was a minor diplomat. He was posted to New York.' She turned back to him, a teasing glint entering her eyes although there was still something sombre about her manner. 'Apparently he was a great friend of your father's.'

'Was he?' Alessandro asked, his tone decidedly neutral. The friendship was not, he thought, anything to recommend the man to him. His father had been for his whole life a reckless, thoughtless and louche dilettante, embarking on one affair after another, never caring whom he hurt in the process.

'Well, that is perhaps a matter of some debate,' Liane conceded. 'But it was how we were invited to your ball. My father lent yours a hundred francs at the baccarat table in Monte Carlo. Apparently he never forgot it. He put my family on the invitation list for several occasions over the years, although this is the first one we have been able to attend.'

'Ah.' He couldn't keep his lips from twisting cynically and Liane nodded slowly in understanding, or perhaps admission.

'My father was a gambler,' she stated quietly. 'He lost all his money at those tables and we moved to Paris and then New York to escape the disgrace. He died soon after.'

He heard the throb of pain in her voice and found it touched him, more than he wanted it to. 'I'm sorry.'

'So am I. If he hadn't lost all his money, he might not have drunk himself to death and then died of liver failure just a year later.' She let out a little sigh, the sound no more than a breath, as she looked away.

'I'm sorry for that as well.' He paused. 'I'm afraid my father shares many of your father's traits. He's still alive, though, living what he sees as the high life in

Ibiza, but he has behaved in a similarly feckless manner all his life.'

She turned back to regard him seriously, her eyes wide and unblinking. 'You're not like him.'

'I thank God for that.'

'That was a deliberate choice you made? To be different?'

Her insight, appreciated only a few moments ago, now caused him a frisson of unease. 'Yes, it was.' He would never be led, the way his father had been, by his lust, or like his mother had been, by her emotions. One had caused his father's dissipation, the other his mother's death. He preferred to remain apart.

'The tabloids are so curious about you, you know.' A smile flirted with her mouth and lightened her eyes to lavender. 'You seem to be something of a recluse, which makes this whirlwind of parties all the more surprising.'

He took a step towards her. 'You've been reading up on me?'

A blush pinked her cheeks as she held his gaze. 'It would be rather remiss of me not to, considering my sister and I are travelling with you for the week.'

'True enough. Well, don't believe all you read in the tabloids.'

Her eyebrows arched. 'So you're not a recluse?'

'Recluse might be too strong a word. I like my own company, certainly, and I often find others' tedious.'

'Then these parties really will be torture for you,' she teased with a small smile.

Right now he was experiencing an entirely different kind of torture, breathing in her scent, watching her eyes turn different shades of twilight, the way her chest rose and fell with each breath. Why was he so affected by her? It was both alarming and annoying, to feel such an instant and overwhelming attraction for someone he barely knew. Even now his palms itched with the desire to reach for her, draw her to him slowly, so slowly...

'I only intend to stay long enough at each one to generate the publicity needed,' he stated, banishing the provocative images from his mind.

'You do sound like a cynic.'

'That's because I am one.' His voice came out rougher than he expected and she blinked, startled. Alessandro was not sorry. As entertaining as it could be to chat and to flirt, he wanted Liane to have no misapprehensions about who he was. What he was. Like she claimed—although he didn't know whether to take her at her word—he didn't believe in the fairy tale. At all. And he refused to give her or anyone else a moment's hope about it, no matter what attraction was springing to life between them.

She held his gaze a moment longer, as if weighing the truth of his words, and then she moved away from him, towards the door that led to the adjoining room. 'What's in here?'

Alessandro came to stand behind her as she opened the door. 'The bedroom,' he said and she shivered slightly, as if she'd felt his breath ripple over her skin. She stood there for a moment, surveying the wide double bed piled high with pillows in varying shades of gold and cream silk. Alessandro stood behind her, close enough that if he bent his head he could have brushed a kiss to the nape of her neck. He eased back.

'What a lovely room,' she remarked after a moment, her voice low and husky, and he wondered if she too were imagining the scene that could be so pleasurably played out there. She started to close the door.

Alessandro caught it with his hand, his fingers brushing hers so she stilled, her body tense, practically vibrating. For a second Alessandro remained with his hand touching hers, the air seeming hushed, expectant. It would be so easy to turn and take her in his arms…

But, no. He was mad to think this way. He *didn't* think this way. He never let himself be led by his emotions or desires. Restraint was his watch word. He couldn't let Liane Blanchard change who he was.

'You should see the bathroom,' he told her, drawing his hand back from hers. 'It's even more luxurious.'

'Oh?' She glanced back at him, her expression veiled, and he enjoyed the way her eyes both widened and darkened, the slight parting of her lush lips—he noticed every reaction, no matter how tiny, and felt the answering flare of both need and desire in himself. Did she feel it too? He thought she must, but her face was as blank and lovely as a marble Madonna's. What was she hiding—and how much?

'Come and see,' he murmured and placed his palm near the small of her back, letting it hover questioningly for a moment, which she answered as she moved forward, slow enough that he was able to keep his hand there, and he was almost fiercely glad. He felt

the warmth of her skin through the thin cotton of her
sundress, burning his palm, firing his senses. Surely
she felt the same pull of attraction. He wanted her to,
even though he knew he wouldn't act on it. But this
couldn't be in his own mind, his own body. She felt it
as well, no matter how carefully veiled her expression.

Slowly, savouring every moment, he guided her towards the bathroom and with an unsteady hand she
opened the door.

'Oh, my.' Her voice came out in a breathy rush as
she surveyed the room—the sunken whirlpool tub for
two, the gilded mirrors on the wall, the pillar candles,
the crystal chandelier winking above. 'How...deca-
dent.'

'Isn't it, though.'

He hadn't meant to sound sour, but she noted it and
it clearly broke the mood as she stepped away from
his hand with a questioning look. Just as well, he told
himself.

'Did you not design it yourself?'

'No, this jet belonged to my father. I usually prefer
to travel by regular aeroplane but, considering the na-
ture of our travels, it seemed both more sensible and
ecological to use a private jet on this one occasion.'

'Your father was a man of decadent tastes?' Her
gaze swept slowly over him, seeking, finding.

'You could say that.'

'Another way you're not like him then, I think.'

'I'll thank you for the compliment, although I'm not
sure how you've discerned so much.'

'Everything about you is restrained.' He blinked,

startled and a bit unnerved by her assessment. 'As if you're always keeping yourself in check. As if you have to, as a matter of principle.'

He managed a laugh, although he was shaken by her perceptiveness. That was exactly how he felt. Never give in to the yearning he sometimes felt because it was weakness. Never let himself be used. 'I'm not sure that's a compliment.'

'I admire a certain amount of restraint.' She paused. 'My father certainly didn't have it, more was the pity for him.'

'And you're not like your father either, are you?' he returned.

'Well, I'm not a gambler.' She let out a small, sad laugh. 'But to be honest I wouldn't mind being like him in other ways—a bit more fun and carefree, able to enjoy life. People loved being around him. I did.' She paused. 'He was a bit like Ella, and she's not even related to him.'

Alessandro didn't reply for a moment; he knew he didn't fully understand the grief she felt for a man who had clearly wasted so much of his life. He refused to feel such emotion for either of his parents. 'So Ella was the daughter of your mother's second husband?' he surmised.

'Yes, Robert Ash. They married when my sister Manon and I were in our early teens.'

'Ella mentioned she doesn't get along with your mother.'

'That would be putting it mildly.' Liane looked away. 'That's not Ella's fault, though.'

'Then is it your mother's?' he asked, curious as to what was making her look so sorrowfully pensive.

'She can be a difficult, prickly sort of person.' She turned back to face him. 'What about your mother?'

Briefly he thought of the woman he'd called mother for a handful of years; his blurry memories were of her drunk or passed out, shrieking or weeping or causing a scene, certainly nothing to dwell on—or to miss. And yet, shamefully, he had. He thought of the last time he'd seen her…throwing clothes into a suitcase, barely looking at him. He'd been eight years old, tearful, begging… *Please, Mamma, please…*

'She left when I was eight,' he told Liane in a clipped voice. 'I don't remember much about her.'

'Left?' Pity flickered in her eyes and he tensed, hating that he was its object. Why had he said as much as he had? It was an odd sharing of confidences they were having, secrets drawn from them almost reluctantly, as if they were compelled to share their souls with each other. Now he really was being fanciful. He had no idea why he was talking like this with Liane Blanchard. Why she affected him so much, both physically and emotionally. It was alarming. It was intoxicating. It needed to stop.

'Yes,' he confirmed dismissively, deciding it was time to put an end to the conversation. 'And then she died when I was eleven.'

'I'm so sorry.'

He shrugged. 'I moved past it.'

'Does anyone move past that sort of thing?' she mused. 'My father was a gambler and a wastrel, but he was fun and he loved me. He…accepted me as I am. I still miss him.'

'Then you have finer feelings than I do.' And, judging by the even more sorrowful look on her face, that pithy remark had revealed more about him than he'd meant it to.

'I'm still sorry,' she said quietly. 'As I would be for any little boy who lost his mother. Ella lost her mother when she was a baby—did you know?'

'It didn't come up in conversation.' They'd kept their chat light and easy, which was how he suspected both of them liked it. Yet here he was, spilling secrets with Liane. It didn't make *sense*…and yet it did.

'Well, it's something you have in common.' She spoke as if she were reminding herself of something, and Alessandro wasn't sure he liked it. He realised he didn't particularly want to be thinking of Ella just now. Liane slipped past him, back into the bedroom, her slender figure moving gracefully past the bed piled high with pillows and silken sheets—and for a second Alessandro could picture her there, lying languidly among the pillows, the spill of her white-gold hair like spun silk against the smooth sheets, her eyes at half mast, her body…

At the door she turned back to him, her expression carefully blank. 'Ella will be wondering where we are,' she said, and it seemed almost as if there was a warning in her words.

Shaking his head as if he had to wake himself from a dream, Alessandro followed her.

CHAPTER FIVE

'ISN'T THIS *AMAZING*?'

Ella held her arms out as she twirled around the centre of their hotel suite, her hair flying out all around her. 'I've never, ever seen a room like this before.'

'Well, Rossi Hotels are meant to be the epitome in elegance and luxury,' Liane reminded her with a laugh. Even though she wasn't twirling around the room like a ballerina, she was similarly impressed, even stunned, by the sumptuous suite they'd been given—a living room with a wraparound terrace, a dining room and kitchen and two enormous bedrooms with en suite bathrooms that were the most luxurious Liane had ever seen—sunken tubs, waterfall showers and more marble and crystal than she'd ever seen outside of Versailles.

'I feel like I'm living in a dream.' Ella flung out one lithe golden arm. 'Pinch me.'

'Very well,' Liane replied with a laugh and gave her sister a light pinch that had her squealing melodramatically.

'Ouch!'

'You know that didn't hurt.' Liane moved past her

to the French windows overlooking the terrace, the palm tree-lined boulevards of Los Angeles spread out before them, the Pacific Ocean a blue crescent in the distance. She stepped outside, resting her hands on the wrought iron railing of the balcony as she breathed in the hot, dry air, so different from New York's summer mugginess.

'You aren't angry with me, are you?' Ella asked as she joined her on the terrace.

'Angry?' Liane repeated in surprise. 'No, of course not. Why would you think such a thing?' She was never angry with Ella; it would be like being angry with a kitten. Still, she could see her sister looked worried as she studied her face.

'I don't know,' Ella told her. 'You've seemed a bit distant since we got off the plane.'

Had she? Liane forced a reassuring smile. 'I'm just tired. This has all happened so fast, my head is spinning.' Which was true enough, even if there were other reasons for her quiet. That conversation with Alessandro on the plane had left her feeling unsettled, as if someone had, very gently, pushed her off balance and she was struggling to right herself again.

She didn't know why he'd spent so much time talking to her, or if she'd been imagining the sensual currents she'd felt flowing between them. When he'd put his hand on the small of her back all her senses had sprung to life, her whole body twanging with awareness and need. It had been shocking, to feel so much from one little touch. To *yearn* so much.

But there was no way, she told herself, that he could

feel the same. If he was flirting with her at all, and she wasn't even sure he was, then that was all it had been—just for fun, a light amusement to while away the journey. Except he didn't seem that sort of man, to amuse himself with other people's emotions. By his own admission, he was restrained, even a recluse, someone who eschewed parties and socialising for hard work and solitude. Why would he tease her like that?

Or had she really been imagining all of it, and his gestures had been born of nothing but mere solicitude? But why seek her out, why ask her about herself, her family? It had almost been as if he wanted to get to know her, even to care. Her ever circling thoughts were making her head ache. She had to stop thinking about him, second-guessing every look, every remark…

'Yes, I know what you mean,' Ella agreed, bringing Liane back to the present. 'But it's an adventure, isn't it?' Her smile was playful but her eyes were still full of worry. 'You're not sorry I asked you along, are you, Liane? You know I couldn't do this without you.'

'I'm not sorry, but are you?' Liane asked, managing to bring another smile to her lips. 'I don't want to cramp your style with Alessandro.'

'Oh, yes, Alessandro.' Ella rolled her eyes. 'He's almost *too* handsome, isn't he? So dark and brooding.' She gave a little shiver. 'I don't know whether he scares me or bores me, to tell you the truth. A little of both, I think. The two of you were gone for quite a long time on the journey.' Her eyes narrowed speculatively. 'What was that about?'

'He was just showing me the plane.' Liane heard

how nervous she sounded. How silly she was, to think it meant anything. 'Being a gracious host, I suppose.'

'A gracious host,' Ella mused. 'Or something.' She slid her phone from her pocket. 'I thought for today's post I'd do a little video story of our trip—I took a photo on the plane, looking out the window, and then I'll do another one getting ready for the party. And then a shot of the ballroom at its most elegant, with Alessandro brooding away in the background—I don't want to give away too much at the start, keep everyone guessing. What do you think?'

Liane glanced down at the artful shot of the blue sky from the plane window, sunlight on clouds, and then another of Alessandro, gazing down at his pile of papers. Brooding indeed. 'I think it looks wonderful,' she managed, doing her best to squash that absurd pang of jealousy—and over what? 'But it's what Alessandro thinks that matters.'

'Unfortunately.' Ella sighed. 'I can't believe he doesn't even have any social media accounts.'

'I don't have any social media accounts,' Liane reminded her. As a teacher, it had been advised for her not to have any, and she wasn't interested in what seemed like a rather shallow world anyway.

'You guys are actually perfect for each other,' Ella told her with a speculative little look. 'Both of you old-fashioned stick-in-the-muds.'

'So that's how you see me.' Liane tried to sound laughingly wry, but she feared a little hurt came through. Did Ella really think she was that boring, that old? *Was* she? As for her and Alessandro being perfect for each other... Ella had clearly meant that as a joke.

'Oh, you know it isn't, not really,' Ella assured her. 'Come on, let's pick out our dresses for tonight. Alonso has a designer friend who lives in LA and he's sent half a dozen dresses for us to choose from. We're both going to look stunning, I promise. Alessandro won't take his eyes off either of us.'

Forcing a smile, Liane let herself be carried away on her sister's enthusiasm and forced the pinpricks of hurt she'd felt at her offhand comments from her mind.

The dresses had been delivered to Ella's bedroom and she unzipped them from their garment bags one after the other, oohing and ahhing over each creation. 'Aren't they stunning?' she exclaimed. 'You'd look amazing in the emerald, Liane. Try it on.'

'I don't think so.' Ella could carry off a gown that was slashed down to the navel and up to the thigh, but she certainly couldn't and she had no intention of trying.

'Come on,' Ella pleaded. 'You'll look amazing, Liane. You have a lovely figure when you choose to highlight it. Don't be such a fuddy-duddy all the time.'

So she was a fuddy-duddy as well as an old-fashioned stick-in-the-mud, Liane thought wryly. Well, what did it matter? She could never be like Ella—fun and carefree, traipsing happily through life, drawing people to her like bees to honey. She'd always known that, and so why should she even try?

'I'll stick with the dress I brought with me, thank

you very much,' she told her sister firmly. 'It's perfectly suitable.'

'You don't mean that blue monstrosity of your mother's?' Ella exclaimed in horror. 'Liane, you *can't*. You'd look like…like my maiden aunt or something. We're at a party in *LA*, for heaven's sake—'

'So?' She hadn't really wanted to wear that old dress—she'd only brought it as a desperate backup—but some stubborn streak made Liane tilt her chin, decided now. She *was* a stick-in-the-mud after all. 'It's the only one I have.'

'What about the purple dress that I lent you—?'

'It had to be returned, as you know.' None of these fabulous gowns were theirs to keep. All of this life, she thought, was a mirage, disappearing in mere days. It would be good for her to remember that. 'I'll be fine in that dress, Ella. I'm not the one here for the publicity photos, remember. I don't really need to go to the ball at all.'

'Not go?' Ella's jaw dropped and she snapped it shut. 'Of course you're going. I need you there.'

'You didn't need me last time,' Liane reminded her. 'I barely saw you the whole evening.'

'Still, this is different,' Ella insisted. 'People will be taking photos…they'll be watching more now. I might do something stupid. You know how I can be.' She reached for her hand. 'I need you, Liane. Please.'

Liane couldn't help but soften. 'Don't worry, I'll go,' she promised, squeezing her sister's hand. She'd go even if she didn't want to, not any more, and she wasn't even sure why. Was it just because of how Ella's thoughtless remarks had rankled, or because she was tired of her supporting role? Ella would naturally be by Alessandro's side, chatting and laughing, flirting and making him fall in love with her, and where would she be? Standing in the corner as usual, but at least it wouldn't be in one of these fabulous dresses that would surely make her seem as if she were trying to be the belle of the ball who absolutely wasn't. The last thing she wanted was anyone's pity, the ugly stepsister who tried too hard. If she had to be a wallflower, Liane thought resolutely, then she might as well look the part.

Another evening, another event. There was no point checking his watch because the party hadn't even begun yet. And if he wanted the publicity to work, he was going to have to stay more than his usual fifteen minutes. Alessandro took a sip of champagne as he glanced towards the doors of the mirrored ballroom of Rossi's Los Angeles Hotel, a modern building of glass and steel, but one that still promised old world luxury and elegance. Where was Ella? And, he wondered with an even greater impatience, where was Liane?

He hadn't seen either of them since they'd arrived at the hotel, when they'd gone to their suite while he'd checked in with the local management. He'd done his best to focus on the work at hand but, irritatingly, his mind had kept drifting—not to Ella, who had kept up a steady stream of chatter all the way from the airport to the hotel, exclaiming about the blue sky and the palm trees and the YouTubers who apparently lurked on every corner, but to Liane, who had been quiet and withdrawn, her face turned to the tinted window of the limo.

She hadn't looked at him once and he'd found it annoyed him, a fact that then caused him even more annoyance. He didn't want to be affected by anyone, and certainly not a little mouse like Liane Blanchard. Except she *wasn't* a mouse, even if sometimes she seemed as if she liked to act like one. Why—and how—did she slip under his skin the way she seemed to, without even trying? Why did he care what she thought, what she was feeling? Why, even now, could he remember the exact shade of her eyes, the tiny freckle at the corner of her mouth?

It was all so ridiculous. He was here to do a job, perform a function, and then return to Rome and the more important business he had there. The last thing he needed was a distraction—or a temptation in the form of a woman whose lavender eyes he couldn't get out of his mind.

'Alessandro!'

He turned at the sound of Ella's musical trill. She looked stunning, and yet his gaze was already moving past her, searching the empty corridor.

'Where's Liane?'

'She's still getting ready, but I didn't want to be late. I wanted to take some shots of the ballroom—look.' She brandished her phone, but Alessandro could barely be bothered to scroll through the photos she'd taken.

'So you approve the post?' Ella asked as she slipped her phone back into her tiny beaded bag. 'Or do you even care?' There was a hint of amusement in her voice that had Alessandro's gaze snapping back to her laughing one.

'Yes, I approve.'

'Oh, good. And here I was, worried that you'd be sticking your nose in too much, telling me how to do my job.' She raised her eyebrows as she eyed him thoughtfully. 'Right now I get the feeling you couldn't care less about any of this. Or me.'

'I leave the social media expertise to you, naturally.' He smiled tightly. 'Wasn't that the arrangement?' His gaze moved past her yet again, to the doors. Guests were beginning to trickle in, waiters circulating with trays of champagne and canapés, the music starting up. *Where was Liane?*

'Now I do believe it's time for you to sparkle,' he told Ella. He took her arm, smiling in greeting at an online entrepreneur he'd met in passing a few months ago along with his latest girlfriend, a Hollywood starlet, who was already starting to gush. He could already tell this evening was going to feel like for ever, every minute ticking by like an hour. And where the hell, he wondered again, was Liane?

An hour passed, every minute feeling endless, just as he'd known it would. Ella, at least, was in fine form, chatting and laughing and tossing her curls for the camera, while Alessandro did his best not to look as distracted and bored as he felt. He still hadn't seen Liane and Ella must have noticed, for as she plucked a second glass of champagne from a passing tray she remarked dryly, 'I saw her slip out to the terrace a little while ago, if you're looking for her.'

'Looking for who?' Alessandro asked, and Ella rolled her eyes.

'Liane, of course. You've been scanning the ballroom all evening searching for her. Fortunately I'm not offended.' Her smile was playful although the expression in her eyes was dangerously speculative. 'Like I said, she's out on the terrace.'

'I wasn't looking for her,' Alessandro replied stiffly. 'I just wondered where she was.'

'Well, now you know,' Ella returned flippantly, toasting him with her glass. 'So you can find her if you want to. You seem to be very curious about her whereabouts, at any rate. And now I'm going to go sparkle some more.' She started off, tossing over her shoulder, 'Good luck with your search.'

He told himself he wasn't going to go out on the terrace; there was no need for him to look for Liane, never mind actually find her. He'd mingle for a few minutes more and then he'd call it a night and do some work up in his penthouse suite. He continued to tell himself that as he walked towards the doors that led out to the wide terrace overlooking Beverly Hills, now shadowed in darkness, and then stepped through them. He scanned the clusters of chatting guests but he didn't see Liane among them. He wasn't actually *looking* for her, he told himself as he wandered amidst the groups of people, greeting and chatting as necessary. He was just mingling, as required.

And then, as he rounded the last corner, he found

her, in an alcove off by herself, her hands on the balustrade as she gazed out at the city, her blonde hair blowing in the breeze.

'Why are you hiding?' he demanded, and she turned to him, no doubt startled by his aggressive tone.

'I'm not hiding. I don't particularly like parties, and two in quick succession are quite enough for me. I just wanted some air.' There was a defensiveness to her tone that both rankled and touched him. He didn't like the thought of her spending the whole evening hiding out here, and why? To get out of Ella's way?

'You've been out here for some time, I should think. I haven't seen you in the ballroom at all.'

Her chin tilted, her eyes flashing. 'Have you been looking for me?' she asked, her tone rather disdainfully incredulous, and he stiffened.

'I merely wondered where you were.'

She shrugged. 'Now you know.'

He stared at her, and she glared back. Why were they arguing? Somehow they'd both been put on the defensive and he wasn't sure how or why, only that he felt off balance, unsettled by her very presence affecting him in all sorts of ways. He should just turn around and walk away, but for some reason he didn't.

'Were you hiding out here for a reason?' he asked and she shrugged, still defensive. 'You belong at this party as much as Ella does,' he said, feeling his way through the words, and Liane gave him a sceptical look.

'No, I don't, and in any case I don't want to be.' She hesitated, and then said with an attempt at a laugh, 'Never mind ridiculous shoes, you must realise this dress is even more ridiculous.' Her lips turned up in a forced smile. 'In fact, it's ugly.'

He glanced down at the dress and had to concede that, even though he hadn't noticed before, the dress left something to be desired.

'It may not be the latest fashion,' he allowed, 'but if you don't like it, why are you wearing it?'

She let out a huff of weary laughter as she turned back to the view, her slender hands resting on the railing. 'I'm not really sure.'

'Was there something else? Ella assured me that your wardrobe was taken care of—'

'*Her* wardrobe. I could have worn one of her fashion designer friends' dresses, it's true, but they didn't suit me, and I'd just look silly wearing something plunging to my navel and slashed to my thigh.'

Alessandro's blood heated at the thought of her wearing such an outfit, but he kept his expression neutral as he answered, 'If you cannot find a gown to suit you, then we must buy one. We'll go shopping tomorrow, before our flight leaves for London.'

She turned to him, her eyes widening in surprise. 'What? No.'

'Why not?' Alessandro was baffled by her resistance. 'There's time, and you need to be suitably attired.' And, he knew, he wanted to spend time with her. Buy lovely things for her. *See her in them...*

'Fine,' Liane countered, her chin tilting up. 'I can pick out my own dress, then.'

Alessandro found he didn't particularly care for that notion. 'Nonsense. You don't know the city or its boutiques, and as I'm the one who invited you on this trip it is my responsibility to make sure you have all that you require. We'll go together.'

She stared at him for a long moment, her eyes dark and troubled, her body stiff with tension. 'Don't feel sorry for me,' she warned him at last.

'Feel sorry for you?' he repeated, his eyebrows rising in surprise. 'Why would I feel sorry for you?'

Liane simply shook her head. 'I might not be as glamorous or beautiful as Ella, but I don't need to be your pity project.' She started to move past him and he caught her arm.

'Liane, that is not what this is about. I don't pity you. If anything...' He hesitated, not wanting to reveal too much about what he felt. Hell, he didn't even *know* what he felt, and he certainly didn't want to think about it too much. But he did want to take her shopping tomorrow, he realised. Quite a lot. 'Ella is starting to give me a headache,' he said at last. 'All that chatting and laughing and tossing her hair. It's exhausting. To tell you the truth, I'd rather be out here on the terrace as well.' *With you.* He swallowed down the words. He had no intention of admitting that much, even to himself. It wasn't as if he *needed* her...or anyone.

A small smile flirted with her mouth and then slipped away. 'You made a rod for your own back with all these parties.'

'I suppose I did.' He let go of her arm, even though he didn't particularly want to. 'Now, tomorrow. Meet me in the lobby at ten o'clock in the morning. That will give us a few hours before we have to leave for London.'

'And Ella? Should she come too?' she asked, and he realised how little he wanted Ella to accompany them. He'd been envisioning a day spent together, just the two of them, Ella nowhere to be found.

'If she needs some new dresses, she's welcome to come along, of course,' he replied after a moment. How could he say anything else? And really, perhaps it was better if Ella did come along. His feelings for Liane Blanchard already felt too complicated, too much. He'd been acting decidedly out of character, doing and saying and thinking things he didn't normally, and all because of this beguiling woman. It unsettled him for all sorts of reasons, and yet he didn't need any distractions from the business at hand and he certainly had no intention of taking this fascination he felt for her anywhere.

And yet he still found he was looking forward to tomorrow.

CHAPTER SIX

'WHERE'S ELLA?'

The abrupt question had Liane pausing mid-stride as she headed towards the doors of the hotel lobby, where Alessandro was waiting, looking as devastating as always in a navy-blue suit, his close-cropped hair still damp from a shower, his brows drawn together in a frown as he surveyed her.

'She said ten o'clock was too early for her, so she's sleeping in.' Liane tried to keep her voice light as she stood in front of him, her insides wobbling like a bowl full of jelly. She'd been fully expecting Ella to come along for this excursion and serve as some sort of protective barrier between her and Alessandro. With Ella chatting and laughing, Liane wouldn't have to talk to Alessandro, or feel like a fool in his presence—the way she had last night, when she'd admitted she had nothing to wear, or at least nothing she was brave enough to wear. All right, perhaps it had been a silly, stubborn thing to do, to wear that ugly old dress, but it had felt like a strange sort of protection at the time. Easier to be a wallflower than to try to step into the spotlight, but she had no intention of explaining that to Alessandro.

And now here he was, staring at her with that same sort of critical assessment he had last night, as if she were nothing more than a problem to solve. It made her want to shrink right inside herself and disappear. The fizzy flirtation she'd felt on the plane, when they'd chatted alone together, when she'd felt his interest like a warm balm on her skin, now seemed like a surreal step out of time. Clearly she'd been imagining those so-called currents flowing between them. She'd *thought* she had been, she'd certainly feared it, but she knew the leaden certainty of it now. Everything had been in her mind—her silly schoolgirl hopes as ridiculous as those stupid shoes.

Now, standing in front of him, trying not to fidget as he scowled down at her, she felt the full weight of his disapproval, or perhaps just his indifference. His face was expressionless, his eyes shuttered.

'Very well,' he said after a pause, his voice clipped. 'My car is waiting.'

Silently Liane followed him outside to the waiting limo. Ever the gentleman, Alessandro opened the door for her first and with murmured thanks she slipped inside, sliding along the sumptuous leather. Alessandro joined her, closing the door and taking out his phone to text a few messages. Liane turned to look out of the window at the palm trees and pink stucco buildings blurring by as they rode in silence for the few minutes it took to arrive at what looked like one of Beverly Hills's most exclusive boutiques, its frosted glass window hiding the elegance within.

'Why is no one else here?' she asked, instinctively letting her voice fall to a whisper as a sophisticated woman in a silk blouse and pencil skirt ushered them inside the empty boutique. The place had remarkably few clothes, just a few curated outfits draped on blank-faced mannequins or padded hangers, the walls papered in silk and a few velvet chaises and sofas scattered tastefully around. Even the air smelled expensive, a subtle scent of bergamot and vanilla.

'Because I arranged for us to have the place to ourselves.' Alessandro spoke as if this were a normal thing to do. Liane couldn't help but be struck by how different their lives were, their whole *selves*. It made her even more certain that she'd been imagining any spark between them. Why would a man who could commandeer shops and fly by private jet have any interest in a poor plain Jane like her? As Alessandro positioned himself on a divan of grey velvet, scrolling through his messages, Liane couldn't help but feel he'd already dismissed her from his mind.

'She needs at least three evening gowns,' he told the woman who was hovering nearby.

'I don't!' Liane protested. Three…! She'd never had so many dresses.

Alessandro lifted his head to give her a questioning look. 'There are three more evening events. You need a dress for each one.'

'I can wear the same one—'

'Your stepsister's social media is already starting to

do what it was meant to do. You're likely to find yourself on the front page of something, and you don't want to be wearing the same dress.' He shrugged and then turned back to the assistant. 'Three, please.'

'What it was meant to do?' Liane repeated, excitement warring with unease at the thought of finding herself on the front page of anything. 'What do you mean?'

'Some newspapers have picked up the story. There has already been a request to feature the New York hotel in a lifestyle magazine, and the concierge there has told me reservations are on the increase.'

'That's…that's wonderful.' She studied his face, all harsh planes and angles, his gaze trained on his phone. 'Isn't it?'

'Of course.' Another shrug, barely a twist of one powerful shoulder. 'Now, are you going to try some things on?' He gave the sales assistant a pointed look and she immediately sprang to attention.

'Yes, of course, Mr Rossi. I have already selected several outfits for Miss—'

'Blanchard.' Her name came out in something like a snap. He gestured to the dressing room, which was almost as big as Liane's bedroom back in New York. 'Then let's get going.'

Liane retreated into the dressing room, closing the door behind her with a firm click. Why was he being so terribly terse? She'd told him last night that she didn't need a dress, or if she did, he didn't need to come with her to shop for it. So why was he now acting as if this was the hassle to end all hassles? This had been his idea, not hers. She'd almost, for a second, thought he might enjoy it, but she realised now how ridiculous a notion that was. How ridiculous all her silly romantic notions had been.

Her fingers trembled as she unbuttoned her blouse, the sales assistant waiting with a gown in aquamarine silk that flowed like water over her arm. She wasn't just annoyed or even angry, Liane realised as she slipped on the dress, although admittedly she was both of those. She was *hurt*. When they'd been on the plane she'd known their conversation—and those delicious currents—hadn't *meant* anything, but some stupid part of her had still believed, or at least hoped, that Alessandro was interested in her, if only a tiny, tiny bit. Now she knew he wasn't. She was nothing but an inconvenience to be dealt with, and impatiently at that. Everything had been in her imagination or, worse, she realised as a new, awful possibility occurred to her, done out of pity. What if he'd given her attention simply because he felt sorry for her? A pity project, indeed, just as she'd said last night. The thought made her stomach roil unpleasantly. She might be mousy but she didn't want to be pitied for it. She wouldn't let herself be.

'Well?' Alessandro called out. 'Let's see.'

Liane barely glanced at her reflection in the mirror. 'It's fine. You don't need to see it.' She had no desire to parade herself in front of him. This whole morning was excruciating enough.

'I want to see what I'm buying,' Alessandro replied mildly enough, but Liane still gritted her teeth.

'Fine.' She yanked open the dressing room door to glare at him, her hands on her hips, wanting him to see the extent of her ire. 'Satisfied?' Her breath came out in an unsteady rush as her angry gaze met his—and then saw the heat flaring there.

'I wouldn't say I'm *satisfied*,' he replied slowly, and Liane's toes curled, everything in her clenching at the innuendo. Was this yet more pity? Throwing her a bone? She couldn't bear it.

'But it suits?' she asked, striving to keep her voice steady. The gown was Grecian in style and covered her from neck to ankles in gently pleated folds, but underneath his considering gaze she felt nearly naked. It wasn't an unpleasant feeling—far from it. As he continued to look at her she felt achingly aware of her own body, his sweeping gaze seeming to burn everywhere it lingered. Senses stirred. Nerves tingled. And heat flowed through her in a molten, honeyed stream. Why was he looking at her this way? Was he teasing her? Toying with her—or did he mean it? The man was *impossible*.

'Yes, it suits. Certainly.' He held her gaze and she had to turn away with effort.

'Fine. Then I will get this one, and thank you for it, but nothing else.'

'But—'

'No.' She spoke firmly, more firmly than perhaps he'd ever heard from her before. She had her limits. 'Only this.' She turned back to him and saw his heated gaze had turned narrowed and considering. 'I don't need you to buy me things,' she told him. 'And I don't want to be your pity project.'

His eyebrows rose towards his hairline. 'Not that again—'

'Only this,' she said again, fiercely this time. Then, as the sales assistant murmured that she would go ring it up, she turned back into the dressing room, her heart thudding at having forced a confrontation. If his attentions had been born of pity then she wanted no more of them. At least she'd made that clear.

She reached for the zip on the back of her dress—and realised she couldn't reach it. She arched her back, stretching her arm till her shoulder socket felt as if it would be dislocated, and still she couldn't manage to grasp the tip of the zip. *Damn.*

Reluctantly she opened the dressing room door. Alessandro looked up from his phone, eyebrows snapping together. 'Where has the sales assistant gone?' Liane asked.

'She went to ring up the dress. Why?'

Even more reluctantly, she admitted, 'I can't undo the zip on my dress. I was hoping she could help.'

Alessandro rose from the sofa in one fluid movement. 'I can help.'

Which was what she didn't want. *Couldn't* want. Him touching her. Her melting—and making a fool of herself. She took a quick breath and then nodded, determined not to show her reluctance *or* her desire. 'Thank you.'

She turned around and caught her breath as she felt his fingers at the nape of her neck, gentle, caressing. She stayed completely still, willing herself not to respond—and reveal. She held her breath, not wanting to breathe in the subtle male scent of him, knowing it would affect her. She couldn't bear the thought that he would know how much she responded to him—and that it would amuse him.

His fingers took hold of the zip and gently tugged. Liane remained rigid as he pulled the zip slowly, so slowly, down her back, stopping midway, the fabric whispering against her bare skin, his fingers so tantalisingly close to her flesh.

'Is that enough?' His breath fanned against the nape of her neck and she had to keep from shuddering in response as a molten longing spread through her veins and she nearly swayed.

'Yes, I think so.' Unsteadily she stepped away, turning around, only to have the dress begin to slide off her shoulders. Panicked, she slapped her hands against her chest to keep it from falling off completely.

She glanced up at Alessandro, and now there could be no mistaking the heat in his eyes. He took a step closer and her breath came out in a shuddery rush as his heated gaze remained trained on her. His hand moved to her hip, fingers barely skimming the dip of her waist as if to help her balance, anchor her there. A shudder of longing escaped her as he bent his head and she closed her eyes, her face tilted to his as she breathed in his citrusy male scent.

Was he actually going to kiss her?

Then the sound of clacking heels.

'Mr Rossi...?' the sales assistant called, and then stopped at the sight of them, frozen there together, so close to a kiss. 'Oh.'

Horrified, Liane bolted back into the dressing room and slammed the door in both Alessandro and the woman's faces.

What had just happened?

What had just happened?

Murmuring his thanks to the assistant, Alessandro stepped back towards the sofa, running his hands through his hair as he tried to tamp down on the heated desire raging through his body. His fingers tingled where they'd touched Liane. His lips burned as if they'd already tasted her sweetness and fire. The moment when she'd turned, his hand near her waist, his head bent as he'd breathed in her feminine, flowery scent...

He'd been so close to kissing her.

Ever since he'd first laid eyes on her, he acknowledged, he'd been fighting this relentless attraction. Today he'd been trying to hide his desire with a pragmatic terseness. Last night he'd called himself all kinds of a fool for seeking her out, insisting he take her *shopping*, of all things...

What was happening to him? Why did this slip of a woman affect him so much, make him say and do things he normally never would? He was a man who prized control, restraint, caution—all the things his own father hadn't. The last thing he wanted to do was lose his head over a woman, any woman. And he wasn't even going to *think* about his heart.

The door to the dressing room opened and Liane stood there, dressed in the plain top and skirt she'd worn before, her cheeks flushed but her expression composed. Just.

'Thank you for the gown,' she said stiffly as the sales assistant came forward with the dress swathed in a garment bag, draped over her arm. 'I suppose we should be heading back to the hotel.'

'We need to have lunch.' The words popped out before he could think them through, surprising them both. He glanced at the sales assistant. 'Thank you,' he said and took the dress.

'I can eat lunch in my room.'

'There's a little bistro near here where I've eaten before, on business. I'm sure they'll have a spare table.'

Liane didn't reply and Alessandro sent a quick text to secure the reservation. It wasn't until they were back in the limo that she spoke, her face angled to the window so he could see her profile—the porcelain curve of her cheek, the delicate line of her jaw. 'I don't understand you,' she said quietly.

'What is there to understand? We're hungry, so we'll eat.' He slid his phone into his pocket, determined to make things simple and not think about the welter of emotions churning inside him.

'You know that's not what I mean.' She turned to face him, her expression grave, her chin tilted at that determined angle. 'Don't you?'

Alessandro stilled, doing his best to keep his expression neutral. He did not want to have the kind of discussion Liane seemed to be angling for, and yet even so he admired her courage in pursuing it. He could tell it cost her, and yet still he couldn't make himself be honest. 'I don't know what you're talking about.'

'You blow hot and cold,' she stated with quiet dignity. 'At first I thought I was imagining it. I was sure I was, because I thought you would never even look at me, especially with Ella around.'

'What does this have to do with Ella?' he asked sharply.

Liane gave a little shrug. 'She's beautiful, charming, funny, charismatic. Everything I'm not.'

'That's not true.'

'I'm not looking for compliments—' she cut across him '—I'm just telling you I don't know how to play these games, if that's what they are.'

He was annoyed, even though already he knew he had to acknowledge the truth of her words. But he didn't play games. That wasn't who he was. 'I'm not—' he began, only to fall silent as she shook her head.

'Whatever it is. You sought me out on the plane, spoke to me as if...' She bit her lip. 'And then in the dressing room, for a moment I... I thought you were going to kiss me.' A rosy blush touched her cheeks but to her credit she held his gaze. 'But last night you seemed annoyed, and this morning you seem angry. I know I'm probably naïve, but you're making my head spin, and not in a good way. I don't know if you're giving me attention as some sort of...of pity but, whatever it is, I don't want it.' She turned back to the window. 'So, if you don't mind, could you please just go back to ignoring me all the time? It's much easier.'

Alessandro was silent, shocked and more than a

little shamed by her dignified speech. He *had* been sending mixed signals, he knew, mainly because he felt so conflicted within himself. He didn't want to feel anything for her…and yet he did. That fact was as undeniable as it was irritating. He barely knew her. He didn't need the distraction. He didn't want the temptation. *The risk.*

The limo had pulled up to the discreet bistro Alessandro had texted and neither of them spoke as he helped her out of the limo and then they walked into the restaurant.

'You're right,' he finally said when they were seated at a secluded table in the corner, menus to hand. She deserved his honesty, at the very least. 'I'm sorry. I have been feeling…conflicted.'

'About me?' Her lips twisted. 'Funny, that doesn't really make me feel any better.'

'I am attracted to you,' he stated baldly. Her eyes widened, her lips parting soundlessly. He found he enjoyed the colour that flared into her face. 'But I don't want to be. And that has nothing to do with you.'

She glanced down at her menu, mainly, he suspected, to hide her expression. 'Doesn't it?' she asked quietly.

'How could you think it did?'

She shrugged, her gaze remaining downcast. 'I'm not exactly about to set the world on fire, am I?' She looked up, trying to smile, determined to be pragmatic, and Alessandro's heart twisted with sympathy. Why did she hold herself in such low esteem? Had she lived in Ella's laughing shadow for too long, or was there something else that had made her doubt herself? He hated the idea that she saw herself like that, but he surely wasn't the man to help her in that regard. 'I never thought I was, you know,' she said softly.

'Falling for someone who sets the world on fire hardly holds any appeal for me,' he told her, keeping his tone wry. 'But this is not about your lack of anything, Liane, but rather a...a discernment in me. I have no interest in pursuing a romantic relationship with anyone. So if I've been sending mixed signals, that's why.'

She stared at him for a moment, her head cocked to one side, her gaze considering, her cheeks still pink. 'Why don't you?'

'Because I've seen the damage romantic attachments can do. Broken hearts and ruined lives hold no appeal for me, and happily-ever-afters only belong in fairy tales. You said you didn't believe in the fairy tale,' he reminded her, 'although I suspect that you really do. But I don't. Not at all.' If he hoped that to be the end of the conversation, he was to be disappointed.

'You don't have to believe in fairy tales to pursue a romantic relationship,' Liane pointed out. 'Not,' she added quickly, 'that that's what I'm suggesting. I'm just making a point. You're taking it to extremes, surely—'

'By romantic I mean falling in love,' he stated. Better to get it all out in the open. 'I am not at all interested in loving someone or being loved back.' Risking hurting or being hurt. He'd seen it all with his parents, the endless cycle of despair and futility, with him at the centre. He had no desire to experience the like again. 'Shall we order?'

'But…' Liane stared at him for a moment, confusion clouding her eyes until realisation dawned and her mouth twisted. 'Ah, of course. You have…other… relationships, don't you? Affairs?' She flung the word at him, her face turning fiery.

Alessandro inclined his head in the briefest of nods. 'I've had certain agreeable arrangements in the past,' he admitted. 'But, returning to my main point, I apologise for sending out mixed signals, and I'm grateful for the opportunity to clear the air. We can now consider the matter settled.' And he would, he vowed, steer clear of her from now on. He'd been foolish to seek her out so much as it was. He was aggrieved to realise he didn't possess the self-control to remain sensible in her presence. Better not to seek her out at all, to ignore her completely, just as she'd said.

The waiter returned and they gave their orders, lapsing into silence as soon as he'd left. The air, Alessandro thought ruefully, didn't feel very clear at all.

'Why not me?' Liane asked finally, a quaver in her voice, and Alessandro blinked at her.

'Why not you?' he repeated, raising his eyebrows. 'Why not you what?'

'Why not consider me for one of your *arrangements*?' Her chin tilted up. 'I never asked for you or anyone to fall in love with me. I told you I don't believe in the fairy tale, even if you doubt me. You have no-strings affairs,' she stated, her voice so very matter-of-fact, even if it possessed a tremble, 'so why not consider me?'

CHAPTER SEVEN

LIANE HELD ALESSANDRO'S gaze as he gaped at her, but only just. She couldn't believe how brazen she was being, but even so she was glad she'd forced the issue. Ever since laying eyes on the man she'd been lambasting herself for thinking about him at all. For indulging a schoolgirl crush and allowing the man to affect her so much, to make her senses spin and her nerves tingle.

She'd had a crisis of confidence, thinking she'd been imagining his response to her, and then an even worse one, fearing he pitied her. Now she was beginning to glimpse the truth, or at least some of it. He simply didn't want to have a casual affair with her. Well, why not?

'Why...why not you?' he practically sputtered, shaking his head as if the answer were too obvious to state.

'It's a reasonable question.' To her credit, her voice didn't tremble any longer, even though her hands did. She hid them in her lap. She could hardly believe she was talking about this—having an affair. *Sex*. And she with virtually no experience of such matters at all. 'So tell me why not.'

'Because.' He reached for his glass and took a sip of water. 'Because you're not the kind of woman a man has affairs with.'

Ouch. She kept her expression bland with effort, her hands still clenched in her lap. 'I'm not?'

'Would you even want such an...an arrangement?' he demanded, turning the tables on her neatly. 'A casual affair with absolutely no future in it? No-strings sex, merely a physical transaction, admittedly pleasurable, that ends when I say it does?' The heat in his eyes as he stared at her in challenge made her lower her gaze.

She'd challenged him out of pique, a momentary boldness that had allowed her to fling the question at him like throwing down a gauntlet, but now she found herself having to consider the matter seriously, a prospect that filled her with both deep unease and utter yearning.

She closed her eyes as she remembered that charged moment in the dressing room when he'd dipped his head, his hand near her waist, the promise of a kiss hovering between them—it had been so little and yet she'd felt so much. How much more would she feel if he'd actually kissed her? If he—

'Liane.' Her name came out sharply. 'Answer me.'

She looked up and saw colour on the slashes of his cheekbones, his eyes glittering fiercely—why? Because of her? *Could he actually desire her?* The knowledge was incredible, wondrous. Powerful. A knowing, catlike smile curved her mouth as a new, dizzying delight raced through her veins. She'd never, ever felt this way before. Never known she could feel it.

'Answer you?' she asked innocently. 'But I'm still considering the matter.' She could hardly believe she was saying the words. She wasn't really considering such a thing, was she? No-strings sex, a soulless, emotionless affair? And yet...*such pleasure*. To feel wanted, to finally, fully step into the spotlight...

Alessandro let out a sound that was close to a groan. 'The question was meant to be *rhetorical*. Of course you don't.'

'Don't I? Why not? I already told you I don't believe in the fairy tale.' She spoke the words with insistence, even though they seemed to ring hollow. She *did* believe in the fairy tale, absolutely, she always had, but in this moment she almost didn't want to. She wanted to flirt. To feel wanted. To have this fiery longing racing through her veins and know, or at least hope, it was racing through his as well. That they could both stoke the flames higher and then finally, wonderfully, sate them...

She glanced at him, eyebrows lifted, meaning to look flirtatious, provocative, but the sudden sober look in his shuttered gaze made her falter, the feminine confidence she'd been enjoying for a few brief seconds trickling away, leaving her feeling empty and embarrassed. The real Liane, looking for a fairy tale that didn't exist, the happily-ever-after that was not for the likes of her.

'But you do,' he said quietly. 'I know you must, no

matter what you just said. You're a woman who…who was made for the fairy tale.'

Her lips parted but no sound came out. Was that meant to be a compliment? It sounded like one, and yet…it was also a rejection, she realised with a sudden, stinging shame. Even if she had practically just said out loud that she'd happily jump into bed with him, Alessandro was telling her he didn't want to. He *wouldn't*.

How could she have been so stupid? How could she have believed for a moment that a man like him wanted a woman like her, someone mousy and shy and uninteresting? She stared down at the table, willing herself not to blush or, worse, cry.

'I believe this conversation has got a little bit out of hand,' he continued lightly, a kindness in his tone that Liane couldn't bear. 'Shall we draw a line under it all and move on—as friends?' He gave her a smile that was full of gentle whimsy and it made her feel like bursting into tears. This was worse than being his pity project. Far worse.

Wordlessly, her throat too tight to speak, Liane nodded. She forced herself to look up to meet his all too compassionate gaze, nodding again as she managed to force out, 'Yes, I think that sounds like a good idea.'

Alessandro hesitated, his grey gaze scanning her face, looking for clues, and Liane prayed she wouldn't give him any. The last thing she wanted was for him to feel sorrier for her than he already did. Somehow she made her lips turn upwards as she leaned back in her seat, eyebrows raised, as if this had all been nothing more than an interesting, theoretical discussion.

'Good,' he finally said, and thankfully the waiter came then with their main courses and Liane could concentrate on her food instead of the awful look of naked pity she'd seen on Alessandro's face.

Somehow he didn't feel that conversation had gone quite as he might have wanted it to. It had been entirely surprising, shocking even, as well as unsettling, to have Liane ask him so directly. *Why not me?*

Why not, indeed?

The truth was, he could imagine all too easily how she would feel in his arms. Her lips on his, her body pliant against his as he plundered her softness, as she yielded it up to him…yes, he could imagine it very well indeed. But the truth was, he'd meant what he'd said. All his affairs had been conducted in an almost businesslike fashion: two people agreeing to use each other's bodies for pleasure. It was cold-hearted, yes, but it had worked. No emotions engaged, no possibility of feeling exposed or hurt, of sending wrong signals, of making it more than it was.

But the thought of having such an affair with Liane was…*wrong*, on a fundamental level. Wrong and distasteful and definitely not something he wanted, strangely enough, considering the desire currently racing through his veins, setting his blood on fire.

She wasn't a woman to be trifled with, to use as he felt like and then dispense with when he was done, even if she agreed with what he already knew would be the undoubtedly, overwhelmingly pleasurable using.

You're a woman who was made for the fairy tale.

What a cringingly sentimental notion, and yet he'd meant it, absolutely. Even if she didn't believe she did, Liane deserved the fairy tale, complete with the bow-wrapped happily-ever-after ending, and that was something he knew he could never, ever give. He refused to try.

Looking at her closed expression now, her eyes veiled as she focused on her meal, he suspected that she didn't believe he'd meant what he'd said. She persisted in clinging to the exasperating idea that he felt sorry for her, simply because she wasn't like her stepsister. As if anyone needed more Ellas in the world!

Even so, Alessandro was hesitant to disabuse her of the notion. Better they simply move on, as friends as he'd said, and never discuss this again. Because if Liane was meant for the fairy tale, he wasn't. And he had no intention of hurting her by letting her think even for a second that fairy tales were real when it came to him…no matter what her sister was able to show on social media.

He thought they managed, more or less, to recover their equilibrium over the course of the lunch; Alessandro asked her if she'd ever been to London, which she had, and then told her he wanted her to show him some of the sights in Paris.

'I'm sure you've seen Paris dozens of times,' she replied, and he smiled at her, longing to get back some of the connection he'd felt before, if not quite all of it.

'Not by a true Parisienne.'

'I grew up more in Lyon than Paris, but very well.' She shrugged, managed a smile that didn't quite reach her eyes. 'If there is time, I'd be happy to show you some sights, but this trip does seem like a whirlwind.'

'I'm sure we can spare an afternoon.' He would make sure of it. Really, Alessandro told himself, this had all worked out for the best. They could spend time together without any miscommunication or uneasiness, knowing exactly where they stood. He could count her as a friend, and maybe even help her believe in herself a bit more. He told himself he was glad they'd had that conversation, uncomfortable as it had been. It really had made everything easier.

'Where's Liane?'

Alessandro glanced behind Ella, where waiters were prepping trays of champagne for yet another gala, this one at the Rossi Hotel in Mayfair. He was so very tired of these parties, and yet he'd been looking forward to seeing Liane in the gown he'd bought her tonight. Looking forward to it quite a lot, in fact, no matter what he'd told himself about them being *friends*.

'She decided not to attend,' Ella replied with a careless shrug. 'The flight tired her out, apparently.'

'She's had all day to recover.' They'd taken a redeye from LA to London, and he'd offered the jet's bedroom to Liane and Ella, preferring to work through the night and then doze in a reclining chair. There had been very little opportunity to talk during the eleven hours from LA to London and yet now he realised that, even so, Liane had been rather pensive and quiet. Had she been avoiding him after their discussion yesterday? Why,

Get ready to relax and indulge with your FREE BOOKS and more!

**Claim up to FOUR NEW BOOKS & TWO MYSTERY GIFTS –
absolutely FREE!**

Dear Reader,

We both know life can be difficult at times. That's why it's important to treat yourself so you can relax and recharge once in a while.

And I'd like to help you do this by sending you this amazing offer of up to FOUR brand new full length FREE BOOKS that WE pay for.

This is everything I have ready to send to you right now:

Try **Harlequin® Desire** books featuring the worlds of the American elite with juicy plot twists, delicious sensuality and intriguing scandal.

Try **Harlequin Presents® Larger-Print** books featuring the glamorous lives of royals and billionaires in a world of exotic locations, where passion knows no bounds.

Or **TRY BOTH!**

All we ask in return is that you answer 4 simple questions on the attached Treat Yourself survey. You'll get **Two Free Books** and **Two Mystery Gifts** from each series you try, *altogether worth over $20*! Who could pass up a deal like that?

Sincerely,

Pam Powers

Harlequin Reader Service

Treat Yourself to Free Books and Free Gifts.

Answer 4 fun questions and get rewarded.

▶ **DETACH AND MAIL CARD TODAY!**

We love to connect with our readers! Please tell us a little about you...

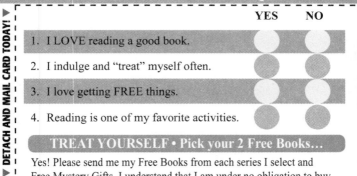

	YES	NO
1. I LOVE reading a good book.	◯	◯
2. I indulge and "treat" myself often.	◯	◯
3. I love getting FREE things.	◯	◯
4. Reading is one of my favorite activities.	◯	◯

TREAT YOURSELF • Pick your 2 Free Books...

Yes! Please send me my Free Books from each series I select and Free Mystery Gifts. I understand that I am under no obligation to buy anything, as explained on the back of this card.

Which do you prefer?

☐ **Harlequin Desire®** 225/326 HDL GRAN
☐ **Harlequin Presents® Larger-Print** 176/376 HDL GRAN
☐ **Try Both** 225/326 & 176/376 HDL GRAY

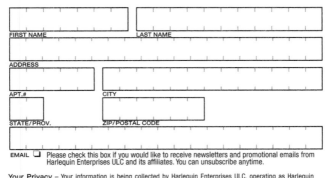

FIRST NAME

LAST NAME

ADDRESS

APT.#

CITY

STATE/PROV.

ZIP/POSTAL CODE

EMAIL ☐ Please check this box if you would like to receive newsletters and promotional emails from Harlequin Enterprises ULC and its affiliates. You can unsubscribe anytime.

HD/HP-520-TY22

when they'd finally cleared the air? Unless, of course, they hadn't.

Ella raised her eyebrows. 'What does it matter? Unless you want her to feature in today's posts? I could take a photo of her, lying in bed with a cloth to her head, you hovering by her bedside...' The smile she gave him was disconcertingly knowing.

'No, of course not.' It was a ridiculous idea, and in any case he couldn't care less about the stupid social media posts, even if they were achieving exactly what he'd intended them to. 'I simply expected her to be here.' Wearing the gown he'd bought for her, that made her look like a Greek goddess come to life—Persephone, perhaps, or the nymphs Echo or Thetis... Good grief, but he needed to get a hold of himself. 'Is she unwell?'

'I think she might have a bit of headache.' Ella cocked her head, looking at him speculatively, one hand planted on her hip. 'If you want, you could go check on her before the party starts. Make sure she's okay.' Her eyes danced. 'I think she'd appreciate it.'

'I'm sure there's no need,' Alessandro muttered, turning away. He needed to stop thinking about Liane. He'd thought they'd reached an understanding, an equilibrium, yesterday afternoon, when he'd made it clear they would not be taking their relationship anywhere, if they even had a relationship, which they didn't, but clearly his brain hadn't got the memo because he'd been thinking of nothing *but* her all day.

Still, he realised as he began to circulate among the arriving guests, he was annoyed and even worried that she'd decided to be a no-show. What was really going on? Was she hiding again, or what if something was wrong? What if she was ill? He frowned, considering the matter. Ella had said she had only a bit of a headache, but what if it was something more? What if she was upset? He'd been a bit brusque yesterday, perhaps. He hadn't meant to hurt her feelings, but neither had he wanted to give her any hope.

The most expedient thing to do, he decided, was to check on her. Five, ten minutes, max, and then he'd be back at the party. He strode through the hotel, mindless of the guests glancing his way. Soared upwards in the lift to the top floor where Liane and Ella were staying in one of the two royal suites, a sudden sense of urgency firing his long strides, the thudding of his heart. Hammered on the door.

'Liane?' he called. There was no answer and he rapped again sharply. 'Liane! Answer the door!'

'I'm coming, I'm *coming*.' Sounding harassed as well as a bit alarmed, Liane flung open the door and stood there, chest heaving, face flushed, as she stared at Alessandro in irritated confusion. She was wearing a soft jersey T-shirt that clung to her slight curves and a pair of tracksuit bottoms that hung loosely from her hips. A single white-gold plait lay over one shoulder and her eyes sparkled like amethysts. She looked, Alessandro thought, irresistible.

'What on earth is wrong?' she exclaimed, at the same time he cut across her,

'Why didn't you come to the ball?'

'Because I'm not Cinderella,' she shot back, 'and I had a headache.'

'But the gown—'

'I'll wear it in Paris. You didn't want me to wear the same thing at each party, anyway.' She shook her head slowly, her expression caught between exasperation and weariness. 'Why are you looking so furious? Just because I'm not downstairs to do your bidding?'

He stared at her for a moment, completely discomfited. He was acting like a *madman.* Why had he raced up here? Why was he so angry? Not with her, he realised, not with her at all, but with *himself.* She drove him crazy...and that was his fault. He was allowing his emotions to be engaged, to be overwhelmed, by this slip of a woman. No matter how they'd allegedly cleared the air in LA, he couldn't get her out of his mind.

'I... I don't know,' he said, his tone wondering, incredulous. This was so unlike him, so unlike everything he prided himself on being. Restrained. Controlled. Level-headed...

'You don't *know?*'

No, he realised, the problem was he *did* know. He knew all too well. And as Liane stood there, gazing at him in confusion, he closed the space between them, taking her into his arms, feeling the rightness of her body against his, slender and supple and pliant. He bent his head, his lips a fraction of an inch from hers, and heard her inhale sharply. Then, with a tiny sigh, she softened against him. And he kissed her.

CHAPTER EIGHT

ALESSANDRO'S LIPS HOVERED over hers for a moment in a silent question that Liane answered as she relaxed into him, revelling in the feeling of his hard, muscular body against hers. His lips brushed hers softly, once, twice, and then settled on them firmly, with deliberate, delicious intent. The fluttering sensation inside Liane's middle exploded into fireworks through her whole body. Her mind reeled. Her nerves twanged. Her senses sprang to life as his arms came around her and her body melted into his.

It was a kiss like no other, although in truth she had precious few to compare it to. Still, it blew them all away, left her reeling and longing for more. One large, warm hand cupped her cheek, another spanned the dip of her waist, fingers sliding up under her T-shirt, warm and seeking on her skin, and still the kiss went on, until Liane felt she saw stars—or maybe she'd swallowed them. Every inch of her was alive, sparkling, incandescent.

She pulled him towards her, revelling in the feel of his powerful shoulders beneath her questing hands, his lips moving from hers to the pulse beating at her throat, her hands now lost in his hair, her mind reeling, reeling…

And then Alessandro, with something like a groan, stepped away, his absence reverberating emptily through every atom. As Liane did her best to straighten her clothes and blink the world back into focus, she saw the colour slashing his cheekbones, the way his eyes glittered. He'd been affected as much as she'd been, or almost. Of that she was sure. She might be naïve, but that kiss, at least, had *not* been motivated by pity, and the knowledge made her fiercely glad.

'Well.' His breath came out in a rush as he squared his shoulders. 'At least we got that out of the way.'

What? For a few seconds Liane could only keep blinking as she fought an urge to laugh in incredulity. *Out of the way?* She felt as if Alessandro Rossi had very much got *in* the way. In her system, her blood, her brain. That kiss had affected her in every way possible; need was still thrumming through her insistently. And now he thought they could move on as if it, along with yesterday's conversation, had *cleared the air*? Was he actually serious? Or was he just trying to convince himself that could happen, because he wanted it to?

She pressed her fingers to her stinging, swollen lips. 'How do you reckon that?' she managed shakily.

Alessandro glanced around the empty hallway and then gestured into the suite. 'May I come in?'

'Yes, of course.'

She watched, everything in her still pulsing with desire and life, as he stepped through the doorway and strode into the suite's luxurious living space, with its velvet sofas and antique art. She closed the door after him and then followed him into the room, standing in the doorway as she watched him warily. He prowled through the space like something caged and restless, before he gave a brisk nod and turned to her, his mind clearly made up, a hard certainty sparking in his steely eyes.

'I'm sorry if I seemed unreasonable. I know I've acted…out of character. But now that we've kissed, perhaps we could see it as breaking the tension. We can put this behind us and move on…' He paused, his words turning weighted. 'If that's what you want.'

If that was what she wanted? Was it her choice, then? Liane gazed at him, nonplussed, wishing she felt more certain about what *he* wanted. The memory of that kiss would stay with her for ever, seared onto her memory, her body, her heart. And it had only been a kiss. How much more would she have been affected if that kiss had gone on and turned into something else? If he'd drawn her by the hand into the suite, into the bedroom, with that wide bed piled with silk pillows, and laid her down gently there, joining her, covering her body with his own…

'You're not interested in an affair, and I'm not interested in anything else,' he stated flatly. 'And, in any case, a few more days and you'll be back in New York, and I need to return to Rome.' He held her gaze, a hint of challenge in his eyes, his voice. 'That's all true, isn't it, Liane?'

She hesitated, a dozen different scenarios unspooling in her mind. She longed to be the kind of woman who could sashay over to Alessandro right now, grab him by his rumpled bow tie and pull him towards her. *That's not quite true*, she'd murmur against his lips, before she kissed him.

He'd take her to bed, and then they'd spend the next few days—or however long it lasted—enjoying each other in every way, ways she didn't even know existed but could heatedly imagine...

And then what?

He'd walk away, just as he'd promised, when he decided. And she'd return to New York with a loved-up body and a broken heart, sick with regret, feeling sad and used, because she knew she would. She wouldn't be able to help it.

'Liane?' Alessandro's voice was low and insistent as he took a step towards her. Her heart clenched, turned over at the intensity of his expression, the planes and angles of his face seeming even harder than usual, more unyielding, more demanding. 'That *is* all true, isn't it?'

'What are you saying? That if I wanted an affair, you'd have one?' She forced the words out through lips that felt strangely numb. She could hardly believe she was asking the question. She was imagining the answer, her body tingling and flaring with desire, aching with the need to cross the small space between them and show him just what she wanted. Or why didn't he make it easy for her and sweep her up in his arms, seduce her so she felt as if she had no choice?

But, no, he was giving her control, and she wasn't sure she even wanted it.

'I'd certainly find it hard to resist you.' His voice was low, thrumming through her, thrilling her, and yet… 'But that's all it would be. A handful of days, and some very memorable nights. I can promise you that, but I can't offer you more. Ever.' He sounded resolute, the words a warning. Clearly he wanted to make sure she would know absolutely how little she was getting. *And yet how much.*

'Yesterday,' she couldn't help but remind him, 'you weren't even offering me that.' He inclined his head in acknowledgement, saying nothing. 'What happened to me being a woman who was made for the fairy tale?' she asked, her voice possessing a ragged, mocking edge. Had he ever truly meant it? Or had he simply not wanted to hurt her, by admitting he could never fall in love with someone like her? Maybe the problem wasn't him, it was her, just as she'd always feared. She wasn't noticeable enough; she wasn't *lovable.*

It was a fear that was rooted in the depths of her, yet one she'd never truly wanted to face. If she was, her mother wouldn't have been so disappointed in her. She'd have found someone by now, twenty-seven years old and no one had even spared her a look…and the one man who had the power to capture her heart didn't want it. She swallowed hard.

Alessandro hesitated, his iron gaze burning into hers. 'The truth is, I want you too much,' he finally said, the words emerging with obvious reluctance. 'If you were willing to take what I can offer, then yes, I would offer it. In a heartbeat. But I want to make sure you understand what I am offering.'

'Yes, I understand that perfectly well,' she assured him shakily. 'You've made it very clear, trust me. A few days and then you're gone. Message received loud and clear.' She tried not to sound hurt, but she could tell that she did by the way his mouth hardened.

'All right, then. You can decide.' He held her gaze, the heat in it both thrilling her and scaring her. No one had ever looked at her that way, with such desire, such naked need. It made her feel strange—powerful and yet helpless at the same time.

'Why me?' she whispered.

'Why not you? Why do you keep acting surprised that I might desire you?'

'Because no one else has before.' She tried for a laugh and didn't quite manage it. 'Because no one else has even noticed me before. Not when Ella is around, anyway, and not really ever. I'm…forgettable.' It hurt to say the words.

'You're not forgettable to me,' Alessandro assured her, his voice a low thrum. 'I haven't been able to stop thinking about you since I first stepped on your toes.'

She shook her head in instinctive denial. 'You don't have to say that—'

'Why don't you believe me? It's true.' He took a step towards her. 'You have this ridiculous insistence on believing that you're not worthy of my attention or desire. Or anyone's. That's simply not true.'

Worthy of his attention and desire, Liane thought, but not worthy of his love. And while Alessandro would tell her that was because of who he was, she couldn't help but think it had to have something to do with her. If she were different, *better*, she would be. Wouldn't she?

Liane took a deep breath. 'And if,' she asked slowly, 'I said I wanted what you were offering?'

His blazing gaze slid to the bedroom and then back to her, making her mouth tingle again in memory. Making her whole body tingle. 'I think you know what would happen next.'

She stared at him for a long moment, so very tempted as well as impossibly torn—but not, she realised with a sinking sensation that was a cross between utter disappointment and weak-kneed relief, torn enough. She wasn't that woman. She never had been. She couldn't offer her body without risking her heart. She couldn't agree to his terms, as much as she longed to.

Already she could imagine it—his fingers threaded through hers as he drew her gently to the bedroom. The heavy-lidded gaze he gave her as he slipped her T-shirt over her head before sliding his large, warm hands down her body, cupping her breasts, spanning her waist, slipping lower…

Her body pulsed with need at the mere thought. How much more intense would the reality be?

And yet she already knew she would refuse. She had to. Alessandro had been right, in a way. She might not be made for the fairy tale, but she still wanted it, and she held herself in enough esteem not to settle for less. And, she acknowledged, just as he did, she didn't want to get hurt, and she knew, she absolutely knew, if she said yes to his offer, she would. She would give him her heart along with her body. She wouldn't be able to stop herself.

He'd walk away without a backward glance, his cold heart completely intact, whereas she would, she knew, be left broken and reeling. Why let that happen, for the sake of a few days' fleeting pleasure, a pleasure that, no matter how incredible, would always be tinted with pain, with loss?

And yet it still hurt, almost unbearably, to force the words she knew she needed to say. 'I guess we got it out of our system, then,' she told him, and she saw his expression become shuttered, like a curtain coming down, veiling all that heat and desire. 'Because you won't risk more, and I won't settle for less.'

'Fine.' His voice was clipped as he gave one terse nod. 'That was what I expected.'

'I'm sorry.' She didn't know why she said it, except that was how she felt. Sorry that it ended here, that he wasn't willing at least to explore the possibility of more. That he had already decided she wasn't worth it. In some ways they barely knew each other, and yet she already knew she could have fallen in love with him if he'd let her. She would have tumbled as hard and fast as Ella ever had, if not harder. Faster. And that, she knew, was the danger she had to avoid. Because a few days would break her heart right in two.

'Don't be sorry,' he told her brusquely. 'It's better this way, really. And in any case, there's only a few more days left of this trip. After that we'll never see each other again.'

Was that supposed to make her feel better? She nodded jerkily. 'Right.'

A silence stretched between them, heavy with the possibilities of what could have been. Candlelight burnishing bare skin, the sensuous slide of silk, of lips and limbs, bodies tangled, joining...

No. It was better this way. It had to be.

'Goodnight,' Alessandro said, and then he turned on his heel and was gone.

There was no need to feel as disappointed as he did, Alessandro told himself as he headed back to the ball. As devastated. He hadn't actually expected Liane to agree to his offer of a brief, no-strings affair. Hell, he hadn't really been expecting to offer. It had taken him by surprise, just as that kiss had taken him by surprise. The intensity of it, as well as the sweetness. The aching need, along with the sense of completion. *At last.*

No. It hadn't been like that at all. It had been a kiss, nothing more. One simple kiss with a woman who happened to set his body on fire. Fine. Sexual chemistry was a proven fact. He could get over it because now, just as he'd said, and Liane had agreed, they'd got it out of their system.

Yeah, right.

He was going to have to believe that, or at least act like he did, if he was going to get through the next few days. Part of him was already longing for the moment when he'd never have to see Liane again and deal with the irresistible temptation she provided, while another, greater, part shied away from such a thought.

Focus.

As he stepped out of the elevator he heard the tinkling of laughter, the clink of crystal, and knew he should go back into the party. Smile, chat, pose. He couldn't think of anything he wanted to do less.

He was a man of determination, he reminded himself, never tossed about or led by his emotions or desires. He'd seen his father run after every woman who caught his fancy, throwing himself into one relationship after another with a passion that bordered on obsession. He'd near ruined his business in the process and even now, at sixty-five years old, living with another mistress whom he insisted was 'the one', he was restless, unhappy, always looking for more. Alessandro had never seen him any other way. He wouldn't be like that. Not for Liane, not for anyone.

Setting his jaw, he turned and walked into the ballroom.

The next morning, under a bright summer sky, they boarded the jet for Paris. If he'd been apprehensive about seeing Liane after their kiss, he shouldn't have been, Alessandro soon saw, she'd smiled at him coolly and taken her usual seat, diagonal to him, opening a book without a care in the world. It seemed as if that kiss *had* got him out of her system.

Why did that thought annoy him to the extreme?

'An American news channel wants me on their breakfast programme,' Ella announced as they took off, waving her phone in excitement. 'Can you believe it? They'll conduct it by video—they're calling it "The Prince of Manhattan's Mystery Princess"!'

'That's a ridiculous title,' Alessandro dismissed. 'I'm descended from a duke, not a prince.'

'Surely you're not much of a mystery?' Liane interjected as she looked up from her book. 'They must know exactly who you are, Ella, from your social media profile, as well as the publicity photos that have been taken during the parties.'

Ella's eyes danced. 'You haven't looked at the posts at all, have you? Either of you.'

Alessandro glanced at Liane, who was looking as uneasy as he now felt. He'd looked at them a little, he conceded, sparing a glance for Ella's phone once in a while when she showed it to him. All he'd seen were artful shots of ballrooms and dresses, champagne glasses and shoes.

'What are you talking about?' he asked, an edge to his voice. 'What is the big mystery?'

Silently, a catlike smile curving her mouth, Ella handed him the phone.

The first thing he saw was the social media account was anonymous—its name was simply *The Glass Slipper*, the profile pic a close-up of the original shoe, lying on the steps. All the photos, he saw as he scrolled through, were artful, mysterious—a tray of glasses, light from a chandelier glinting off crystal. A shot of Ella's reflection as she looked in the mirror, but so the viewer only had a glimpse of blonde hair, a diamond earring, the smooth curve of her cheek. The balcony of the London hotel, one slender, pink-tipped hand on the balustrade.

The captions were intriguing, as well as admirably smooth advertising for each Rossi hotel:

Who has captured the Prince's heart in the heart of LA?

Pining for the Prince with a view of Mayfair...

She'd even included some shots of the suites, captioning each one with something provocative yet whimsical. Each post had garnered thousands of likes, hundreds of comments. And, it seemed, an interview on American television. As silly as it could seem, Alessandro had to admit there was a certain artistry to it all.

'You're a talented photographer,' he told her as he handed back the phone, 'as well as marketing consultant. I might hire you in that capacity, if your social media career turns out to be unsatisfying.'

'Oh, I doubt it will,' Ella told him.

'Still,' Alessandro continued with a frown, 'they must know it's you, considering the photos we've had taken together.'

Ella shrugged, that catlike smile still playing about her lips. 'We'll see,' she said.

It was less than an hour to Paris and Liane immersed herself in her book the whole time, so Alessandro kept to work. As Paris came into view, Liane put down her book and looked out of the window, a faint smile touch-

ing her lips. This was her home, Alessandro couldn't
help but think. Had she missed it?

As they were exiting the plane, he laid one hand
on her arm and she turned to him, eyebrows raised
in query.

'I'm still looking forward to you showing me the
sights,' he said, and her smile, when it came, was like
a starburst of sunshine.

'Of course. I'll be happy to.' Still smiling, she moved
past him, down the ramp, leaving Alessandro feeling
strangely unsettled. Yes, he thought rather moodily,
they had certainly cleared the air.

CHAPTER NINE

'SO WHERE SHALL we go first?' Alessandro asked as he joined Liane in the lobby the next morning for a day of sightseeing. 'Or are you going to surprise me?'

'I'm afraid you might be disappointed,' she told him with a little laugh. 'The sights I'm showing you are, I fear, somewhat ordinary.'

'But it's still Paris,' he said, smiling as he took her arm. Liane tried not to react to the feel of his strong forearm twined with hers. Since she'd turned down Alessandro's offer, she was doing her best to act unfazed. Cheerful, even, and certainly unaffected, although it felt like the performance of a lifetime. Still, they both knew where they stood. That had to be a good thing. She kept telling herself it was, even as she'd lain awake all night, staring at the ceiling and trying not to imagine Alessandro taking her into his arms, his mouth on hers, his hands on her body...

At least this felt like a good thing, to walk out into the summer sunshine of her favourite city in the world, the pavements sparkling with dew, the sky a fresh, breezy blue, the Eiffel Tower piercing its brightness in the distance.

'I've become rather used to spending my nights in a penthouse suite,' she remarked teasingly as they headed down the Champ de Mars. Alessandro had offered the use of his limo and chauffeur but Liane had insisted they walk, in order to experience the city better. 'It's going to be a shock when I return home.'

'You live with Ella in New York, yes?'

'Yes, in a townhouse by Central Park. It's lovely, so I can't really complain.'

'But?' Alessandro filled in, his crinkled gaze scanning her face with a half-smile.

'But it's not mine. Ella's father, my stepfather, left it to her, with the proviso that my mother and sister and I could all live there as long as we wanted.' She shrugged. 'And considering the astronomical rents in Manhattan, it makes sense to stay there, especially on my teacher's salary. But one day…' She paused, embarrassed, unsure whether to continue, but then Alessandro prompted her again.

'One day?'

Why shouldn't she tell him? She'd made it clear, and so had he, where they both stood. That could give them a certain freedom to be honest, to be real, and she suddenly found that she wanted to be so. 'One day I'd like a house in the country,' she told him with a smile and a purposeful swing in her step. 'It would need to be old, a rambling kind of place with hidden corners and twisting stairs and funny, poky rooms.'

'Poky rooms?' He raised his eyebrows and she laughed.

'Not in a bad way. Just…the kind of house that has a personality, feels alive. One that keeps surprising you with its secrets.' They'd turned onto the wide, sunny avenue of Rue de l'Université, the chestnut trees that lined the boulevard providing some welcome shade from the bright summer sun.

'And what would you do in this house?' Alessandro asked, and once again Liane hesitated. Did she really want to share her dreams, private and precious as they were? But why shouldn't she? They were friends, after all. They'd both made that so abundantly clear. Surely that freed her to tell him her fairy tale, the one she'd dreamed of since she'd been a little girl, the one she was still waiting for. She knew, with a deep, certain instinct, that he wouldn't laugh at her for it.

'I'd have cats and dogs and children,' she informed him with blithe determination. 'Several of each, preferably. And a garden. A big vegetable garden, and pots of herbs, lavender and thyme and sage, and flowers too. Big, blowsy roses and lilac bushes… I love the smell of lilac. It was at the house where I lived as a child, in Lyon—it makes me feel sad and happy at the same time, somehow. I want a house that smells of lilac the whole spring long.' She glanced at him uncertainly, realising she was babbling, but Alessandro, gratifyingly, looked arrested.

'Tell me more,' he said.

'And there'll be a big kitchen, but cosy too, with a range and a big, square oak table and a sofa somewhere, the squashy kind you curl up on with a dog or a cat or…or a lovely little toddler.' She looked away, blushing, because she realised she was imagining a serious, dark-eyed boy a lot like Alessandro, one who had that same glinting smile. 'And it would have a wood burner too, for winter nights or frosty mornings…'

'It sounds as if you've imagined this house in detail,' he remarked dryly.

'Oh, I have.' She let out a wobbly little laugh. Embroidering her dream house, her dream life, with all of its wonderful threads had been a very pleasant pastime over the sometimes lonely years, from when she'd been a little girl to far more recently.

'And what about the man in this scenario?' Alessandro asked mildly, his hands in the pockets of his trousers as he sauntered along. 'I assume, with the children you mentioned, there is a man of some description?'

'Oh, yes.' Her cheeks warmed and she kept her gaze straight ahead. 'There's a man.'

'And what is he like?'

Alessandro's tone was neutral, but Liane's skin still prickled and her lips tingled as she remembered their kiss. The house was one thing, but did she really want to talk about this with him? The man she hoped she would love one day. Well, she thought with sudden, heady recklessness, why not? He'd made it clear it would never be him. That didn't mean her fairy tale prince wasn't real, or at least wouldn't be one day.

'I don't have as many preconceived notions about him,' she told him. 'I don't mind what he looks like or does for a job, or anything like that. What matters is that he is kind, and honest, and loyal. And he must have a sense of humour. That's very important.'

'And like cats and dogs, I presume. And children.'

She gave a little laugh. 'Well, yes.'

'And of course he must want to live in this pastoral paradise with you.'

'That, too.' She slid him a sideways glance, uncertain of his dry tone. Was he mocking her? Or merely cataloguing her rather ridiculously long list of requirements? 'It is just a dream,' she reminded him quietly, and he stopped right there on the street, laying a warm, sure hand on her arm.

'Dreams are important.' His silvery gaze blazed down at her as his hand tightened briefly on her arm. 'Don't give up your dream, Liane.'

Why, she wondered, did that feel like some sort of warning? 'What about you?' she asked. 'What are your dreams?'

He removed his hand, shaking his head as he kept walking. 'I don't have dreams. Not like that, anyway.'

'Too jaded?' she teased softly, although his words made her feel sad. 'Too cynical for daydreams?'

He gave a small, rueful laugh of acknowledgement. 'Perhaps.'

'And what made you so?' she asked as she fell into step alongside him. 'Was it your parents, their difficult marriage?'

'That was certainly the start of it.'

'Tell me about them.' She longed to know more about him, but she also wondered if, for Alessandro, speaking of them would be similar to lancing a wound.

That prized restraint, that all-important self-control, she suspected, hid a depth of emotion he was afraid to feel or even acknowledge to himself. Perhaps she was being fanciful, but she felt it all the same.

Alessandro didn't speak for a long moment, and Liane began to wonder if she'd pushed too hard. Maybe they should have stuck to daydreams. Then, finally, the words emerged slowly, chosen with care, offered with reluctance.

'They were the fairy tale, at the start. Italian nobility and a movie starlet, their wedding was covered by all the European newspapers. Everyone thought they were perfect together.' He paused, his mouth tightening. 'All I remember is the fighting—and the tears.'

'Oh, Alessandro…'

He shook his head, as if to stay her words. 'My father had affairs. He couldn't resist a woman, still can't. My mother was beside herself with jealousy, and in her misery she drank and wept and raged. And fought him, doing her best to make him hurt, the way she was. They were always at each other, doing their best to draw blood, metaphorically speaking, but sometimes literally as well.' He paused, his gaze distant. 'I remember lots of shouting and tears, broken glass, slammed doors.' A short sigh escaped him. 'They loved each other, and that love caused them only pain.'

'It doesn't have to be that way for everyone,' Liane felt compelled to remark quietly. 'Surely you can see that, Alessandro?'

'I haven't seen many, if any, examples of a relationship that worked,' he replied brusquely. 'And I have no desire to try myself.' He gave her a fulminating glance. 'Don't make this about that, Liane.'

Chastened, she nodded. 'I'm sorry. Tell me more.'

He shrugged. 'What more is there to say? They made both their lives a misery, and mine as well. Sometimes they'd trot me out at parties, proof for whoever was wondering that their marriage wasn't the disaster it really was, a point of pride, I think, considering their celebrated start. They wanted to present a united front, and I was the only way they knew how to do that.'

Liane's heart twisted hard with sympathy. She'd had her own childhood challenges, with her mother's critical sternness and her father's tragic death, but she'd never had to deal with the kind of confusion and heartache Alessandro clearly had. 'That must have been awful,' she said quietly.

'It was. One of the reasons I don't like parties.'

'And it ended when you were eight, you said? Your mother…?'

His expression became shuttered and he angled his head away from her. 'She finally left. I suppose she'd had enough of my father's affairs.' He paused, as if he were going to say something else, but then he merely looked away, his lips compressed.

'You're an only child?' she asked gently.

'Yes, of my parents. I have a younger half-sister, the child of my father's third wife—or is it fourth?' He glanced back at her, wryly this time, although there was a grim set to his mouth. 'She lives in Umbria. I'm planning to see her after all these parties.'

'You're close?'

'I wouldn't say close, but I want to make sure she has a childhood that's better than mine was. She's only fourteen.'

'And what about your father? You told me he's in Ibiza. Why is he not with her?'

'Because he's hopeless with any sort of responsibility. She lives with her mother, Christina. As far as my father's wives go, she's not so bad. Better than some. Better than my mother's second husband, anyway.'

'What was he like?'

Alessandro shrugged. 'I only met him once, when she was leaving m...my father.' The slight hesitation made her think he'd been going to say *me*, and her heart ached for him, for the small boy he'd been. 'He was quite a bit younger than her, clearly with an eye for the main chance. He lasted all of nine months before he left her, taking most of her money. She tripped from man to man after that, and died in a car crash when her latest lover was at the wheel, and over the limit.'

'Oh, Alessandro.' Liane couldn't keep the dismay and compassion from her voice. 'I'm so sorry.'

He shrugged again, looking away. 'She was out of my life by then. I could barely remember her.'

'But still...' Liane hesitated, and then said quietly, 'I'm not surprised you're cynical about love, considering. I suspect I would be too, if my parents had been like that. If I'd encountered so much heartbreak and tragedy along the way.'

'Perhaps.' He quickened his step, giving her a smile that didn't quite reach his eyes. 'But why are we talking about such a gloomy subject? It's a beautiful day, and we're in Paris. Let's enjoy it, and not lose ourselves in the past.'

Why had he told her all that? Alessandro wondered. He normally didn't talk about his parents; he hated even thinking about them. Remembering their regrettable marriage took him back to his own lamentable childhood—hiding upstairs, wincing at the sound of screaming, only to have one of the house staff appear at the door.

'You're wanted downstairs, Master Alessandro.'

And he'd go, he'd always go, filled with dread and, worse, that tiny, treacherous flicker of hope.

Maybe this time it will be different. Maybe I'll be able to get them to stop fighting...

No, he certainly didn't want to think about those days.

And yet, he acknowledged, Liane drew the past out of him, all his secrets and hurts, the way a doctor drew poison. He felt unsettled for having said all that, but he also felt, in a strange way, better. It had been something of a relief, or perhaps an emotional bloodletting. Either way, he was ready to move on.

'So you haven't actually told me where we're going,' he said, and Liane gave him a glinting smile.

'My favourite museum in Paris, the Musée d'Orsay. It has the best collection of Impressionist paintings. And then afterwards I thought we could stop by the Orangerie, where Monet's water lilies were installed. You step inside a curved room and feel as if they're completely surrounding you.' She paused, a small, sad smile touching her lips. 'My father used to take me there.'

'Did he?' Alessandro couldn't help but sound diffident, although he realised he might be biased, when he considered his own father and all his shortcomings. 'You told me before you've missed him.' Although he'd wanted to stop talking about the past, he'd much rather talk about hers than his.

'Yes, I do. I know he was both a gambler and a drinker, and my mother despaired of him, but...' She sighed, a soft breath of sound. 'He was so *fun*. He could make you feel like you were the centre of his world, and whenever I was with him I felt as if I could have an adventure. Now that I'm older, I recognise how destructive some of his behaviours could be. But as a child...he felt magical to me. After he died, I retreated a bit, I suppose.'

'It must have been hard.'

She nodded. 'Yes, we'd only been in New York a short time, we hardly knew anyone and I didn't actually speak English very well.' She grimaced. 'There were some challenging years.'

'Why didn't you move back to France?'

'Because my mother had already met Ella's father, Robert Ash, and there was nothing to go back to in France, anyway. My mother's parents were dead and my father had lost all their money.' She sighed. 'It all sounds terribly tragic, but it wasn't so bad, especially after Ella came to live with us.'

Had Ella been someone to love, Alessandro wondered, in a life that seemed sadly devoid of it, since her father's death? He wasn't normally one to over-analyse emotions, but he sensed a similar kind of loss in Liane that he felt in himself. They just happened to have reacted to it very differently, with her insisting on the happily-ever-after dream and him refusing to believe in it.

They reached the museum and by mutual, silent accord they both stopped talking about the past and instead focused on the present, touring the museum's incredible offerings, although Alessandro enjoyed watching Liane's face light up as she looked at a painting more than seeing the actual art on the walls—Monet, Cezanne, Van Gogh—such masters had nothing on the play of emotions in Liane's violet eyes, her porcelain skin. The pink flush that came onto her cheeks, the sparkle in her eyes, the way she cocked her head to one side as she considered a painting or sculpture—Alessandro felt as if he could have watched her for ever.

And it was risk-free, he reminded himself, since they'd both made their positions clear. Strange, how that thought did not comfort him very much.

After the Musée d'Orsay, they went to the Orangerie, Liane leading Alessandro by the hand into the centre of the room where the massive canvases of Monet's water lilies hung all around, laughingly insisting he close his eyes.

She guided him to a bench, her hand soft and slender in his, and then whispered, like it was Christmas, like it was magic, 'Open your eyes.'

He did, and for a second all he saw was a blur of colour—lavender and green, flower and water and sky, all of it surrounding him. For a second, fancifully, he imagined he was in Liane's fairy tale garden, with the blowsy roses and the lilac bush. He could almost smell their sweetly haunting scent. The dogs were in the distance, there was a child toddling on chubby legs, Liane's laughter floating on the breeze. He felt...*happy*, a joy springing up in him that made a smile come to his lips.

Then he blinked the paintings into focus and found that the smeary beauty of Monet's lilies in their endless misty garden was nothing compared to the vision that, for a second, he'd conjured from the yearning depths of his own mind.

'Well?' she asked, squeezing his hand. 'What do you think?'

'I... I think it's beautiful.' He felt strangely emotional, and he suspected it had nothing to do with Monet. She was still holding his hand, as if she'd forgotten, and he didn't want her to let go. He certainly wouldn't. He turned to her and for a second he longed to cup her face in his hands, draw her to him. Forget all his stupid resolutions. He cleared his throat. 'Thank you for showing them to me.'

They had lunch at a little café near the Tuileries Garden, washing mussels and crusty French bread down with a carafe of white wine, and then walking slowly through the gardens, resplendent in sunshine, drinking in the day.

'So what will you do when you return to New York?'

Alessandro asked as they wandered along, past the placid pond of the Grand Carré.

'Nothing much, I suppose.' Liane gave a little laugh that somehow sounded resigned. 'School doesn't start back up till September, and I don't have any holidays planned. I'm working on a translation of Rimbaud's poetry for a textbook. If I can, I'll finish that.'

She spoke pragmatically, but Alessandro thought it sounded rather lonely—and sad. 'And what about your farmhouse in the country?' he asked, and she gave him a startled, uncertain look.

'What about it?'

'How are you going to find it, languishing in the city, translating poems?'

'I'm not expecting to find it,' she said after a moment. 'Not like that. I won't stumble upon it like…like the Prince did the bewitched castle in *Sleeping Beauty*, to name another fairy tale.' She let out a laugh that held a note of longing.

'You won't? How, then?' He wasn't sure why he was pressing the point; did it matter to him if Liane found her fairy tale? The answer came instantly, absolutely. *Yes.* Yes, it did.

'I suppose… I suppose it will find me. Somehow. Some day…' Self-conscious now, she gave him a wry yet troubled look. 'Don't worry, I'm well aware life doesn't actually work like that and I should probably go out and find it myself, hack down the thorns and storm the castle, as it were. But I've never been particularly adventurous.'

No, she'd simply supported her stepsister in *her* adventures. Of course he was entirely the wrong person to tell her to go have her adventures. Cut down the thorns, storm the castle, find the Prince and kiss him senseless. How could he tell her any of that when he hadn't done it himself? When he'd told her, and convinced himself, that he didn't believe in fairy tales, that love was nothing but pain and trouble and not worth even finding, never mind fighting for?

And yet, as they started back towards the hotel, he still wanted the fairy tale for Liane. Even though the thought caused him an almost agonising twist of jealousy and longing, he hoped she found her happily-ever-after…even if it could never be with him.

CHAPTER TEN

'Where have you *been*?'

Ella clucked and shook her head, her hands on her hips, as Liane came into the hotel suite. She'd just left Alessandro down in the lobby, with a bittersweet smile and a promise to wear the dress—his dress—tonight. She'd had the most marvellous day, she thought, full of laughter and fun, of both companionable silences and enjoyable conversation, of strolling through Paris on the arm of the most beautiful man...yes, it had been wonderful, but it had filled her with an impossible longing too. Alessandro was *not* part of the fairy tale. She had to keep reminding herself of that again and again, because the more time she spent with him, the more it felt as if it could be possible—if only in her own head. Her own heart.

'I told you I was going sightseeing with Alessandro,' Liane replied as mildly as she could.

'I didn't think you'd be gone for so long—'

'It's only four in the afternoon. The party's not till seven.' Liane gazed at her sister in concern. 'Is something wrong?'

'No, far from it. Something's *right*.' Ella looked as if she were bubbling inside. 'Something's really right. I had that online interview this afternoon—'

'Oh, yes, how was it?' Liane exclaimed, a pang of guilt assailing her at the realisation that she hadn't even remembered that was happening; she'd been too wrapped up in her day with Alessandro.

'Oh, it was fine.' Ella waved a hand in airy dismissal. 'It's so easy online, you just open your laptop. They wanted to know how I met Alessandro, whether I really was "his Princess", as the tabloids are saying.' She grinned and rolled her eyes as jealousy made Liane's stomach clench. She knew it was all smoke and mirrors, pretence and presumption, but it still rankled. She hadn't let herself look at any of the online speculation, hadn't wanted to see the photos of Ella on Alessandro's arm, knowing how the media would play it, the Prince and the Princess. The fairy tale and the happily-ever-after.

'And what did you say?'

'Oh, I let them wonder, of course,' Ella replied with one of her rich, throaty laughs. 'Can't give the game away! I said I thought there was definitely someone he was interested in, but whether it was me...' she took on a look of wide-eyed innocence as she gave Liane a slow blink '...that I really couldn't say.'

'And they bought that?' Liane returned with a laugh that came out just a bit too forced. 'When you've been in all the magazines, draped on his arm?'

'How many magazines do you think I've been in?' Ella exclaimed. 'It's the *hotel* that's being featured,

Liane, not me. I might be in a shot or two, but that's all. I'm hardly a celebrity.'

Liane stared at her in surprise. 'But the whole reason Alessandro asked you to go along was to give the hotels some publicity—'

'Yes, the *hotels*. And I have, through my social media. But no one even knows it's my account.'

'What?' Liane blinked at her in confusion. 'Why? I mean…you want to be an influencer, Ella! Why would you make it anonymous?' She realised she'd been imagining Ella in every shot, arm snugly woven through Alessandro's, her head on his shoulder as they danced the night away…

Had it not been like that? Had her own tortured imaginings been worse, and far more painful, than the reality?

'Did you not hear me talking to Alessandro about it on the plane?' Ella's eyes danced as, mutely, Liane shook her head. No, she'd tuned out their conversation because she hated how unsettled and, yes, *jealous* it made her feel. She knew their so-called relationship was fake, and she felt relatively certain that Alessandro wasn't interested in Ella, but it still made her feel small and mousy and forgettable to see them together, circulating among the crowds, dazzling everyone. She didn't want to think about it more than she had to.

'Well, the point isn't to make me famous,' Ella explained with a smile and a toss of her head. 'It's to make the hotel famous. Keep people intrigued as well as guessing—'

'Guessing what?'

'Who Alessandro is in love with, of course!'

Liane tried not to flinch.

He isn't in love with anyone, she wanted to tell her sister. *He refuses to be, because he thinks love is somehow damaging, or maybe even dangerous, and he's never, ever going to risk it.*

'And how are you doing that?' she asked, and with a canary-eating grin Ella handed her her phone.

Silently Liane swiped through the images—the artful shots of crystal and candlelight, the glimpse of Ella in the mirror, so it could—almost—be any woman. *The Prince of Manhattan's Mystery Princess.*

'They're wonderfully done,' she told her as she handed back the phone, 'but everyone must know it's you. You're the Instagrammer, after all, and you posted the first shot with that glass shoe—'

'Oh, I keep them guessing,' Ella replied with a smile that bordered on smug. 'Trust me on that.' She slid her phone into her pocket. 'But now onto more practical matters! I can't go to the party tonight, so you have to go in my place.'

Liane's jaw dropped as terror and delight twined tightly together, flared low in her belly. 'What? I can't possibly—'

'Oh, but you can, and you have to. After my interview this morning some French YouTubers got in touch with me. They follow fashion and they want me to feature in some of their videos, wearing some of Alonso's designs. They've only got this evening free, though, so I have to go.'

'But Ella,' Liane protested as a growing feeling of

alarm took hold of her, 'you have a contract with Alessandro.'

'Did I sign anything?' Ella challenged blithely. 'No. And to be honest I think I'm doing him a favour. I've been at every party so far. It's becoming boring. People expect me to be there—the presenter on the TV show who interviewed me thought I was his PA.' She rolled her eyes, pretending to look affronted. 'Far better to focus on you, this new, mysterious woman.'

'Me?' Liane squeaked. She could hardly believe it. She could never be like Ella, basking in the limelight. Everyone would laugh at her, they would think she was being ridiculous... 'No. I can't.'

Ella's baby blue eyes sparkled with challenge. 'Why not?'

'Because...because I'm not the sort of person who steps into the spotlight. Who enjoys it.'

'Then maybe I have to give you a push.'

'No.' Liane shook her head, her hands pressed to her hot cheeks. She hated the thought of being not just Alessandro's object of pity but the whole world's and worse, of scorn. 'No, no, I couldn't, Ella, really.'

Ella stared at her for a moment while Liane kept shaking her head. 'Don't you want to?' she asked finally. 'At least a little? Aren't you tired of standing on the sidelines—not just of a party, but of life?'

'*Ella.*' Liane couldn't keep the hurt from her voice.

'I'm serious, Liane. You live so quietly, never attracting attention, never putting yourself forward for anything or, more importantly, for anyone. When's the last time you even had a date?'

'I'm not like you,' Liane protested. 'I never want to be the centre of attention.'

'I'm not saying you have to be the centre,' Ella replied with a laugh, 'the way you know I love to! But you deserve more than the shadows. I know you think your mother makes my life miserable, and she definitely tries, but she does for you as well. You don't even see it, the way she asks you to fetch and carry for her, how she's always criticising, acting as if you're never quite good enough. In some ways she's harder on you than on me. At least I know she doesn't like me. She's meant to love you.'

Liane opened her mouth and closed it again, shocked by Ella's clear-eyed assessment.

'And I know I'm as much to blame as anyone,' Ella continued frankly. 'I know I take advantage of you without even meaning to. It's so easy to do, Liane, because you're so wonderfully kind and supportive. You're always thinking of other people...'

'Then don't take advantage of me by dropping me in it this evening,' Liane interjected a bit desperately. 'Please.'

Ella planted her hands on her hips, her eyes narrowed. 'Why not?'

'Because!' Liane cried. 'Because I can't do this. I don't know how to sparkle and chat the way you do. Alessandro will be furious—'

'Somehow I don't think he will,' Ella murmured. 'And I'm afraid this is going to be a bit of tough love. I'm going, Liane, and you're doing it. But don't worry, I won't drop you in it.' She glanced at the time on her phone. 'We've got two and a half hours to get you ready and, trust me, we're going to use every minute.'

Liane couldn't believe how ruthless her stepsister could be—not just about insisting she attend the ball on Alessandro's arm, but in preparing her for the privilege. Liane had always known Ella loved her spa days and beauty treatments—some of them rather ridiculous— but she'd never subjected her to them, the way she was now.

'Fortunately I brought my supplies,' she told Liane as she opened a suitcase that was devoted entirely to a vast array of beauty products. 'We'll start with an exfoliating face mask, and then a soothing one, so you won't look like a tomato tonight! I'll do your nails too—goodness, you clip them short!'

'It's sensible,' Liane murmured.

'Oh, let's forget all about sensible, shall we?' Ella replied with a wicked glint in her eye. 'For tonight, at least.'

At some point Liane gave up trying to put up a fight; she'd always known what a whirling dervish her sister could be, although her attentions had never been so singularly focused on her before. She let herself submit to not one but two face masks, a manicure and pedicure, a body scrub and then a host of hair treatments before Ella led her out of the huge, sumptuous bathroom to the bedroom, covering her eyes with one hand as she insisted she did not look in a single mirror.

'Wait till you see the finished product,' she instructed severely. 'I want you to get the full impact.'

'I do have a dress, you know,' Liane told her.

'Oh, yes, I know,' Ella purred. 'Alessandro bought it himself, didn't he? Thank goodness we won't have that blue bag of a dress to worry about.'

'It wasn't that bad…' Liane protested feebly.

'It was *worse*. Absolutely horrendous. Now come here, because I'm going to do your make-up.'

Obediently Liane came, sitting down on a stool and closing her eyes while Ella got out her bag of tricks. 'I don't want to look *painted*,' she began nervously.

'You sound like Belle-Mère,' Ella scoffed as she began to rub some sort of lotion into Liane's face. 'Painted, indeed. What is this? The Victorian age? Pinch your cheeks for a bit of colour? You can wear make-up, Liane, and not look like some sort of wicked woman.'

'I know that,' Liane said quickly. Perhaps she was acting at least a little ridiculous, still stung by old memories.

She did her best to relax as Ella continued with her ministrations and then helped her into her dress and heels, adding some tasteful costume jewellery from her own collection and a final generous spritz of perfume. She placed her hands on Liane's shoulders, steering her towards the mirror, insisting her eyes remain closed.

'I'm afraid to look,' Liane admitted with a shaky laugh as Ella positioned her in front of the full-length mirror.

'Don't be, you're amazing!' Ella squeezed her shoulders. 'Now open your eyes.'

* * *

Alessandro glanced at his watch, his mouth tightening. All around him waiters circulated, guests were arriving and a headache was banding his temples. After he'd left Liane he'd gone straight to work, dealing with various matters on both the investment and hospitality fronts, lambasting himself for taking a day off, even though he couldn't make himself regret it. The day with Liane, he knew, would be one that would stay in his memory for a long time to come. One that would bring a smile to his lips and a poignant sorrow to his heart. A day out of time.

He glanced at his watch again and then looked up, his breath catching in his throat as he caught sight of Liane coming into the ballroom.

She was a vision, enough to make everyone's heads turn, although she hardly seemed aware of the attention, her lovely, tremulous gaze focused on him. Just as he was focused on her, the whole world falling away as he drank in the sight of her.

Her hair was piled on top of her head, a few white-gold curls trailing over her bare, silky shoulders. Her eyes looked luminous, a deep, velvety purple, her lips lush, her skin like the creamiest porcelain, touched with a blushing pink. And as for her figure—swathed in the Grecian-style gown, the fabric rippling like crystalline water over her slender, supple curves. A single sapphire nestled in the hollow of her throat, matched by diamond-encrusted ones at her ears. Her toes peeped out as she walked—silver-spangled heels, another pair of ridiculous shoes. He realised he was grinning as he stretched out one hand.

Her fingers whispered against his as he drew her closer. 'Ella…' she began, and he had to blink because for the last minute at least he'd completely forgotten Ella even existed. 'Ella can't come tonight. I'm so sorry.'

'I'm not,' he said simply, and a smile of incredulous wonder bloomed across her face like the most precious of flowers. 'I'm not at all.'

He heard the murmurs of speculation ripple around the room; no doubt people were noticing his change of escort, his reception of her, and yet he hardly cared. Gossip, rumour, speculation, publicity—none of it mattered a whit in this moment. This evening was for him and Liane.

Was he imagining how the music swelled, a crescendo within him as he took her in his arms and they started to dance, moving together in perfect harmony and rhythm?

'I have two left feet,' Liane warned him, and he shook his head. He wouldn't hear her disparage herself, not tonight.

'You dance beautifully. And you're dancing with me. That's all I care about.'

Her eyes widened as confusion clouded their violet depths, and he knew why she was confused, because he felt it in himself, even as something in him crystallised and became wonderfully clear. Tonight, he decided, was magic. Tonight was a moment out of time, out of reality. Tonight was for them, and neither of them needed to think about the future.

The song finished on a crescendo of strings and Alessandro fetched them both glasses of champagne before they joined some of the other guests. If he'd had any concern that Liane would somehow not be able to handle the endless chitchat—and he realised quite quickly that he hadn't—then they would have been put to rest as soon as she spoke. She wasn't all sparkle and glitter the way Ella was, commandeering a conversation with her energy and wit. No, Liane was quieter, deeper, listening with an intensity that made people feel important, asking questions that were pertinent and interesting. Her French flowed easily, her voice light and musical, and Alessandro's heart swelled with pride and something more. Something like possession.

Halfway through the evening he'd had enough of the crowds and he drew her out onto the balcony, the perfumed night air as soft as silk, the Eiffel Tower a beacon of light in the distance.

'This all feels so unreal,' she said quietly as she grasped the railing, as if she needed to anchor herself to reality. 'I feel as if I need to pinch myself.'

'I assure you, you don't. It's real.' His voice was a low thrum and she turned to him suddenly, an urgent light coming into her eyes.

'Is it?' she asked softly. 'You've been so attentive, Alessandro, so…enchanting. And acting as if you're… you're almost enchanted with me.'

'I am—'

She shook her head, a quick movement. 'Don't,'

she whispered. 'If this is for Ella's social media, or the press, or—'

'Do you honestly think that?' Alessandro demanded in a raw voice. He gestured to the balcony, the empty darkened space. 'Do you see any cameras? Any paparazzi?'

'No...'

'I am not doing this for show. This isn't about any of that, Liane. I couldn't care less about any of it. All of it. I never have.' The words came from deep inside him, a place he hardly ever accessed, where his yearnings had lain dormant for so long. He could hardly believe he was confessing to having them at all, and yet he could not ignore them now. He wanted her. He *needed* her. And he didn't care if she knew it.

'Then why...'

'You've got into my blood,' he said simply. 'My mind. My...' *Heart.* He couldn't say it. Even caught up in the moment, drunk on both her beauty and sweetness, he couldn't let himself go that far. 'I need you,' he said instead, and her lips parted softly in surprise.

It felt like an invitation, and slowly he wrapped his hand around the nape of her neck, his fingers sliding through the silk of her hair. A shudder escaped her in a breath of acceptance. He took a step towards her and she let her head fall back so he was cradling it, her eyes heavy-lidded, her lips lush and waiting.

The kiss, when it came, was soft and slow and languorous, as if they had all the time in the world when he knew they only had this evening. This moment. And still it went on as he traced the outline of her lips, tasted the honeyed sweetness of her mouth, and her arms came around him as she returned his passion, firing his senses and his blood, making him crave even more.

He broke the kiss to press another to her cheek, her ear, her throat…he couldn't get enough. He wondered if he ever would. Her breath came out in another shudder as she sagged against him as if her legs couldn't carry her any more, her fingers driving through his hair.

Alessandro had a primal urge to sweep her up in his arms, carry her through the ballroom like a prince of old with his bride. Somehow he managed to claw back some sanity.

'Stay the night with me,' he whispered against her throat, her mouth. 'Stay the night.'

Her fingers stilled in his hair, her body tensing beneath his. 'Just the night,' she said slowly, carefully, and of course he knew what she was asking.

'I don't know how long it would last,' he admitted in a voice ragged with wanting. 'But I know what I feel for you now and it overwhelms me.' He lifted his head to gaze into her eyes, cradling her lovely face in his hands. 'Please, Liane.' He'd never begged before, yet it felt like that was what he was doing now. He, a man who never asked for anything, who made sure he never needed anyone, was *begging*. It was shaming and freeing all at once, to admit to this need. To need someone this much, when for so long he hadn't let himself.

Liane stared at him, her eyes full of torment, her lips trembling. 'You told me I was made for the fairy tale,' she said after a moment, a catch in her voice, her face cradled in his hands. 'You're the only person who has said such a thing to me, who let me believe that I was. That I could be.'

'Liane…' Already he felt the moment slipping away; what had, seconds ago, felt beautiful and precious now felt sordid and wrong. Had he really been begging her to sleep with him? Had he fallen that low, become that craven? He dropped his hands from her face and took a step away.

'I'm sorry, Alessandro.' She pressed one hand to his cheek and he closed his eyes, resisting the urge to turn his head and press a kiss to her palm. 'It's taking everything I have to say no to you, and the only reason I'm doing it is because I know you have the power to break my heart.' He swallowed hard, humbled by her honest admission, horrified by his own. He'd done the one thing he'd said he never would—been led by his emotions. Let them bring him to this awful place of loss and rejection and *hurt*. How could he have been so stupid?

'I could fall in love with you,' Liane confessed, an ache in her voice as Alessandro struggled to school his features into something cool and implacable. 'I think part of me already has, without wanting to, without meaning to. I'm sorry, for your sake as much as mine. I know it's not what you want. This has happened so suddenly, so intensely. For me, anyway.' She let out a wobbly laugh that held more than a hint of sadness as well as an ache of longing, and it made Alessandro want to take her in his arms again, but he didn't. He wouldn't, now that it was so obvious where he stood. 'I'm not trying to pressure you into offering more than

you can give. I hope you believe me on that. I just…
I just can't give myself to you knowing what you are
willing to offer in return. How little. I… I can't let
myself be hurt like that, and I know I would be. I'm
sorry.' Her voice choked on the last words and before
he could reply she hurried from the balcony, moving
quickly through the crowded ballroom, just as Ella had
a week ago, except this time, Alessandro knew with a
leaden certainty, it was no publicity stunt.

Liane was running away—from him.

CHAPTER ELEVEN

LIANE STARED DOWN at the note, written in Ella's loopy scrawl, with complete incredulity. Her head ached from too much champagne and too many tears. Last night, after the most magical evening she'd ever experienced, she'd come home to the unhappily-ever-after she knew would be waiting for her. Never mind the glass slipper, she'd turned into a pumpkin, or the carriage had, however the old story went. She was back to being hide-in-the-shadows Liane, and she wished she wasn't.

She wished she'd had the courage to say yes to Alessandro, to take what he had to give. Who even knew if it might lead to something else, something so wonderfully more? And, even if it didn't, it would have been more than she'd ever been offered before. Why not risk it?

And yet she hadn't, because she was cautious and careful and *scared*. She didn't leap into life, she didn't have adventures, and she certainly didn't tumble into bed—or into love. She'd managed to escape with her heart intact, but in the cold, dull light of morning she bleakly wondered if it was worth it. She wished she had the courage to act differently...

She gazed down at Ella's note again and slowly shook her head. How could she have done this? A quick, impatient tap on the door had her slipping the note into her pocket. *Alessandro.* She wasn't ready to see him again, not after she'd fled so melodramatically from the ballroom, and after he'd admitted to so much. *Why* couldn't she have said yes? Why couldn't she have taken what he was willing to offer? Could she still? Another tap on the door.

With a quivering sigh, Liane went to answer it.

'You look tired,' Alessandro remarked critically as he stepped into the suite.

Liane let out a shaky laugh. 'I am tired,' she told him, trying for tart and feeling she missed it by a mile. 'Thank you, though, for pointing it out.'

Alessandro gazed at her coolly, completely unapologetic for his criticism. He didn't look tired, she thought bitterly. Freshly shaven, dressed in a three-piece charcoal-grey suit, smelling of citrus, he was as devastatingly attractive as always, powerful and remote, needing nothing and no one. *Utterly unaffected.* This was not the same man who had held her in his arms and pleaded with her to spend the night with him. Liane was already half wondering if that had actually happened, doubting her own recollection in light of this new, hard reality. Perhaps it had been too much champagne and wishful thinking...

'Where's Ella?' Alessandro glanced around the empty suite, Liane's suitcase by the door.

'She's gone,' she replied wearily. 'She left with the YouTubers early this morning, before I woke up.'

'What?' His dark brows snapped together as he stared at her. 'What do you mean, she *left*?'

Liane shrugged, spreading her hands helplessly. 'They're doing some video thing in the south of France. She didn't give me the details, just said she was sorry that she had to go and she thought she'd done enough already, in terms of the hotel's social media.'

You can take care of the rest yourself, she'd written, but Liane wasn't about to say that to Alessandro. She couldn't take Ella's place. She hadn't managed it for a single evening. 'I'm sorry,' she told Alessandro.

'You don't need to apologise,' he replied. 'You are not your sister's keeper.'

Liane remained silent, knowing there was nothing more she could say. Ella should have explained to Alessandro herself, but she'd left that unfortunate task to Liane. Briefly she thought of the playful postscript to Ella's note—*And have fun!!!*

As if.

Right now Alessandro was looking more than a little annoyed, and colder than she'd ever seen him. Last night seemed like nothing more than a dream, a figment of her desperate imagination. And to think she'd been wondering if she should reconsider…!

'What shall we do?' she asked uncertainly while Alessandro gazed dispassionately around the empty room. The last of the Rossi Hotel balls was tonight, in Rome. But without Ella…

'We'll go without her,' he stated flatly, as if the matter was both settled and of little interest. 'After last night's performance, she's not even needed.'

Liane's cheeks heated as she held his cool unaffected gaze. 'What do you mean, last night's *performance*?'

In response Alessandro pulled a tightly rolled magazine out of his pocket and dropped it, without ceremony, on the coffee table where Liane had found Ella's note. She blinked in disbelief as the magazine unrolled and the cover page was revealed—the photo was unmistakably of *her*. Her fleeing the ball last night, the blue folds of her gown streaming out behind her, the crowds parting as she ran towards the double doors like a deer being hunted. Colour touched her cheeks. She looked ridiculous—foolish and frightened, as if she'd had the very devil at her heels.

'But...' Her lips formed the word numbly. 'How did they...'

'We had invited the press there, of course,' he remarked dispassionately. 'And it seemed this was the perfect photo op.'

'Photo op...!' Her head jerked up from the sight of the photo as she stared at him in shocked dismay. 'You can't think...'

'I can't think?' He arched one eyebrow coolly.

'You can't think I left the ballroom for some sort of publicity shot,' she forced herself to say. It seemed laughable as well as horrible—she, mousy little Liane, looking for publicity the way Ella did? And yet Alessandro was looking at her so coolly. 'Do you?' she burst out.

'No,' he answered after a moment, his voice toneless. 'And in any case, this is the kind of publicity we want, isn't it?' He didn't sound particularly enthused. 'Everyone buzzing about who the mystery woman who ran out of the ballroom is. Apparently Rossi Hotels is trending on Twitter.' He sounded bored rather than pleased by this fact.

'Oh…' Liane's mind whirled unhappily. She didn't want to be on the cover of a magazine, or trending on Twitter. There was a reason, she realised, why she'd avoided the limelight. She didn't like it. And right now she wished, quite desperately, that none of this had happened.

'As it is,' Alessandro continued, 'now that you've made the covers of these tabloids, you can finish the job and accompany me to Rome. You were going to anyway, so the matter, really, is negligible.'

He started to turn away and she burst out, 'Is that really what you want?'

'It's just one more day,' he replied with a shrug. 'The day after tomorrow you can fly back to New York and translate your Rimbaud.' He didn't look at her as he strode to the door. 'I'll meet you in the lobby in fifteen minutes.'

As the door clicked shut behind him, Liane sank onto the sofa, her knees watery, her mind spinning. She'd lain awake half the night, her body aching, her lips stinging from when he'd kissed her, wondering if she could possibly be bold enough to tell Alessandro this morning that she'd changed her mind. That she'd take however little he had to give, and be glad. Be ridiculously happy, as a matter of fact.

Thank goodness she hadn't blurted that out the moment he'd come in! He clearly had moved on from last night's tender moment. But why was he acting so cold? The idea that she'd run from the ballroom in order to catch something on camera...why, it was completely absurd. And even if she'd done it, wasn't that what he wanted? It was what he'd hired Ella for, after all. If for Ella, then why not her? Why act as if she'd...she'd *betrayed* him?

And then the penny dropped, a flicker of realisation unfurling inside her, along with a cautious wonder, a tentative hope. Was his irritation over the photo, his remoteness with her, a cover for his hurt? Because she'd run away? He'd asked her to stay the night. He'd kissed her with unashamed passion and framed her face with his hands and he'd practically *pleaded*. That had not been her wishful thinking.

Liane knew he was a proud man, one who did not allow himself to be guided or controlled by his emotions. Who hated the thought of being vulnerable. Was that what was behind his icy demeanour this morning? Or was she ridiculous to hope she'd affected him that much? To hope that he actually cared, if just a little.

With a start Liane realised she'd wasted ten minutes in pointless reflection. She was due in the hotel lobby in just five minutes, and she didn't want to add to Alessandro's ire. Quickly she jumped up and packed the last of her things, throwing tissues, a lip balm and her phone into her bag before she hurried to the door.

'You're late,' Alessandro said shortly as she came breathlessly into the lobby.

'I'm sorry—'

He'd already turned away, walking briskly out of the hotel to the waiting limo. As soon as Liane slid into the sumptuous interior, Alessandro took out his phone and started scrolling.

'Checking the publicity for the hotel?' she enquired tartly and he glanced up at her, the look in his steely eyes veiled.

'Answering work emails, as it happens. I couldn't care less about the publicity.'

'Really? Then why were you so annoyed that I was on the cover of that magazine?' His jaw tightened and she continued, unable to keep both the hurt and hope from her voice, 'I thought you *wanted* publicity. I thought that was the whole point of this—this exercise!'

'It is.' He turned to look out of the window as the Paris traffic streamed, a steel-grey glimpse of the Eiffel Tower visible in the distance. He was closing her out, Liane realised hopelessly, and why should she be surprised? Even if he was acting angry in order to hide his hurt, what did it matter?

Even if he felt something, he didn't want to feel it. The end result was still the same. She turned to look out of her own window, blinking back sudden tears. She'd refused him last night because she hadn't wanted to get her heart broken, so why was she feeling so miserable now? It seemed the end result had been the same for her too, no matter what she'd chosen.

They didn't speak until they were settled on Alessandro's jet, he with his work laid out in front of him and Liane feeling as uncertain as ever. She gazed around at the luxury that had left her speechless just a week ago, and now she was already becoming tired of it. She wanted to go home, to return to what was familiar and safe, and yet at the same time she knew she didn't want that at all. When she finally had to say goodbye to Alessandro, she knew she would be devastated. No matter how hard she'd tried to protect her heart, it clearly hadn't worked.

Alessandro gazed at Liane from the corner of his eye as he did his best to focus on his work. She looked bereft, and he couldn't blame her. He'd been acting like an ass. He should apologise, and he kept meaning to, but somehow he could never find the words. He couldn't bear to admit that he'd been acting this way because her rejection of him last night still stung.

He hadn't meant to plead with her. He never begged, and yet last night he'd wanted her so much he hadn't been able to keep the words from spilling from his lips. *Stay... Please, Liane.* He cringed at the memory, and yet he knew he'd meant it, even if he wished he hadn't.

He'd promised himself a long, long time ago that he'd never beg for someone's attention, their love. He'd never even want to. At least, he told himself, it had been clear that all he'd wanted was her body in his bed. Not her heart. Not her love.

No, never that.

Impulsively Alessandro checked Ella's account to see if she'd posted anything about last night, and he saw, with something he decided was irritation and nothing deeper, that she'd posted the photo of Liane fleeing from the ball. From him. She'd captioned it *Can the Prince find his Princess again?* There were already thousands of views, hundreds of comments.

From the angle of the shot, no one could tell it was Liane. No one, Alessandro realised, even knew who Liane was. Ella was certainly playing up the mystery angle, and the world's media had captured the spirit of the thing. He should be glad, he knew; this was what he'd wanted, a controlled narrative that brought publicity for the hotels. As it was, he was starting to find the whole thing both tedious and distasteful. He didn't want any more of it—not for himself, and not for Liane.

He glanced at her again, taking in the ivory curve of her cheek as she looked out of the window at the azure sky, her gaze shuttered, the downward turn of her lips desolate.

'What are you thinking about?' he asked suddenly.

She glanced at him, startled but also weary. 'That I don't want to go to yet another wretched party,' she replied on a sigh.

'Neither do I.'

Something flickered in her eyes and then was gone. 'For someone who says he hates parties, you've gone to rather a lot of them.'

'An astute assessment.' A faint smile flickered about her mouth and he leaned forward. 'Why don't you want to go?'

'Because I'm tired of parties. Tired of pretending.'

'Were you pretending last night?' The words slipped

out before he could bite them back. At least his tone was cool, repressive rather than pleading.

She gazed at him for a long moment, her eyes as dark and soft as pansies. 'No,' she whispered. 'No... In fact, this morning I was...' She took a breath, let out a little uncertain laugh. 'I was reconsidering my answer.'

His breath caught as he gazed at her, a pulse hammering in his throat as hope unfurled, then soared. 'Were you?'

'Yes, I was. I...' She moistened her lips, lifted her chin. 'I want to be with you, Alessandro. For...for however long you're offering.'

He sat back, his mind whirling, his blood roaring. *She wanted him.*

She nibbled her lip as she regarded him uncertainly. 'You...you haven't changed your mind?'

'Changed my mind?' He swallowed a hoarse laugh. 'No.'

'Then...'

Why, when he finally had her surrender and his victory, did he feel...not disappointed, no, never that, but something almost like...sorrow? It was so strange. He should be expectant, exultant, and instead he was... confused. He couldn't understand it at all.

'Alessandro?' she prompted, a waver in her voice.

'What made you change your mind?'

'I'm tired of being cautious and careful,' she replied, again with the tilt of her chin. 'I want to live. I want to...experience things. Ella has always been telling me to have fun, to be in the moment—well, that's what I'm choosing now.' She met his gaze defiantly, and Alessandro couldn't help but think it was all a far cry from what she'd said she wanted. The fairy tale in all its glory.

Yet who was he to decry her choice, especially when it dovetailed so neatly with what he wanted?

Or at least what he'd thought he did…

'If you haven't changed your mind,' Liane asked with a nervous laugh, 'why are you glaring at me?'

'I'm not glaring.' He gave her a quick smile as realisation unfurled within him. Niceties be damned, Liane had made her choice…and he would make his. 'I was just thinking about what you said. What it meant.'

A blush touched her cheeks, turning them to rose-tinted porcelain. 'Then you…agree?'

'Oh, yes.'

Her smile was both shy and lovely, filled with hope and longing, and it made Alessandro certain, his flickering doubts finally quenched.

'Wait.' He rose from his seat and walked swiftly to the cockpit, issuing instructions to the pilot before returning to Liane. His blood was roaring in his veins, his heart singing with joy. He knew he'd never felt this way about a woman, an affair, just as he knew, already, that it was so much more than that. Even if he'd tried for it not to be. Already, before they'd even touched, it was…whether Liane knew it or not.

She twisted around as he came back into the main cabin. 'What were you doing?'

'Telling the pilot to redirect the flight to Perugia.'

'What…?'

'We'll skip the party in Rome. We've both had

enough of these ridiculous charades, the stares and suggestions. We'll go to my villa in Umbria instead.' He realised he couldn't wait to show it to her—the gardens, the spacious rooms, the sense of home. He wanted to share it all.

'But people are expecting you,' Liane protested. 'They'll wonder why you haven't shown up.'

'Then let them wonder. After last night's photo, they'll think we've run away together.' His blood heated at the thought.

'And do you really want them to think that?' Liane asked in surprise.

'I don't care what they think.'

Her gaze flitted away from his, and then resolutely back again, heat shimmering like gold in their violet depths. 'What now?' she whispered unsteadily.

He chuckled softly as he felt the answering flare of need fire through his body. 'We enjoy the expectation,' he murmured. 'And we drink champagne.'

'Champagne?' She sounded endearingly scandalised. 'It's ten in the morning!'

'So?' One of his staff silently appeared and Alessandro asked for a bottle of Cristal. 'We're celebrating.'

Her mouth kicked up at the corner. 'I suppose we are.'

He sat down opposite her and reached for her slender hand, taking it in his. It felt small and cold as he pressed it between his palms. 'Are you regretting your decision?'

She shook her head, the movement almost vehement. 'No, not at all.'

'You're sure?' He desperately wanted her to be.

'Yes,' she said firmly. 'I'm just nervous.'

'You don't need to be.'

Her mouth quirked wryly. 'You can say that because you've probably wined and dined thousands of women before taking them to your bed.'

'Hardly thousands.' And they faded to insignificance in light of this moment.

'Yes, but this isn't new for you, the way it is for me.'

'It's new for you?' He kept himself from admitting just how new it all felt to him.

'Yes. Newer than…well, newer than anything.' She flushed as she let out a little embarrassed laugh. 'If you know what I mean.'

Alessandro hesitated, startled but, he realised, not entirely shocked by her admission. She had to be in her late twenties, and yet… 'Liane, are you saying you're… you're a virgin?'

'That's exactly what I'm saying,' she replied with an attempt at flippancy that made his lips twitch and his heart ache. 'So you might be regretting your decision, as I'm probably going to be very clumsy and gauche about it all.'

'Somehow I doubt that very much.' No, he realised, he wasn't regretting anything. Rather he felt hugely gratified. *She'd chosen him.* The steward came back with a bottle of champagne, popping the cork neatly before pouring two flutes. Alessandro murmured his thanks while Liane waited, watching him apprehensively.

'Let us toast each other,' he said softly, after the

steward had gone. He handed her a glass and then clinked his with hers. 'To us,' he said, and a smile flitted across her face, curved her lips.

'To us,' she agreed, 'and to now.'

Was that a warning to herself—or to him? Or was she just letting him know that she understood the rules? The trouble being, he realised, that he was somehow managing to forget them all. He took a sip of champagne and then put his glass on the coffee table, realising he could not go a moment more without touching her.

'Come here,' he said, his voice a low thrum, and then, as she fumbled to put her glass down, he reached for her hand and drew her slowly, willingly, from her seat, her lips parting in expectation, her eyes going dark with desire.

'You're so beautiful,' he said softly as she stood in front of him, her body slender and supple and *his*, even before he'd touched her.

'You're the beautiful one.' Gently, but with daring, she rested her hand against his cheek. He closed his eyes, savouring the simple touch. 'I feel as if I'm dreaming,' she whispered.

He put his hands on her slender waist and then drew her down to his lap. A little clumsily, with a breathless laugh, she put her arms around him.

'I don't even…'

'You do.' He cupped her face in his hands as he drew her towards him for a long, lingering kiss. She tasted like champagne, but infinitely sweeter. Already he knew he could never get enough. 'Oh, you do.'

She let out another breathless laugh of wonder as his lips moved to her throat. 'Do you know what you do to me?' he murmured as he kissed the hollow of her throat, one hand cupping the slight fullness of her breast. She was perfect. Perfect in every way.

'No.' Her body arched against his hand. 'What do I do to you?'

'You drive me mad. Make me ache.' He settled her more firmly on his lap and her eyes widened. 'You never have to doubt yourself about that.' He wanted her to know how beautiful she was, how desirable. She never need doubt herself, her allure, again. He could give her that much at least. 'You've been driving me crazy since I first stepped on your foot.'

Her surprised laugh morphed into a gasp as he undid a button of her blouse, revealing the lacy silk of her bra. His lips moved over the ridges and seams and she arched against his mouth. '*Oh…but…you were annoyed with me then.*' She drove one hand through his hair to anchor herself as he continued his explorations, tasting her sweet skin, enjoying her little gasps of pleasure.

'Annoyed at how affected I was.'

'Even then…' Her breath came out in a sigh as he nudged the lace aside, tasted the silky sweetness of her skin.

'Even then.'

Her eyes were dazed, her face flushed as he undid another button, his fingers dancing across her heated skin, daring to go lower. 'Alessandro…'

They'd barely begun and yet already he was aching for her in every way possible. He'd wanted to give her a delectable taste of what was to come, but this sweet, slow torture would be the undoing of him. He settled her more firmly on his lap, pressing into her, feeling her yield.

'*Oh...*' Her eyes widened as she braced her hands on his shoulders and tentatively pressed back against him, gasping softly as pleasure flared hotly through him at the feel of her so intimately against him. Her breasts were pressed to his chest, her thighs splayed across his. He knew he was precariously close to losing control, and he could not have that happen here. He wanted to give her much more than a quick, desperate fumble.

Slowly, regretfully, he eased back. 'That,' he told her huskily, 'was a promise of things to come.'

She let out a breathy laugh as she rested her forehead on his shoulder. 'I feel as if I'm singing inside,' she whispered shakily.

He laughed softly and pressed a kiss to her bare shoulder. Tonight, he thought, would be an opera, an endless aria of pleasure as he made her body sing... and sing...and sing.

A discreet knock sounded on the door of the cabin.

'Signor Rossi?' the steward called. 'We are approaching Perugia.'

CHAPTER TWELVE

LIANE FELT AS if she were walking through a dream. The plane landed and they emerged into the sun-baked heat of an Umbrian afternoon, an SUV waiting to take them to Villa Rossi, tucked among the rolling green hills, while she existed in a daze of remembered pleasure.

Her body was thrumming, all the secret parts of her twanging to life, uncovered and aching, yet with a pleasurable ache as she thought, with a frisson of thrilled wonder, of how Alessandro had touched her...and how he would touch her still.

He looked unaffected as he chatted to the driver who greeted them, yet Liane caught the slight flush still on the hard planes of his face, remembered the throb of his body against hers, and it made her blood heat and her heart race all over again. There had been no doubting his desire for her, of that she was sure.

And is desire enough?

She ignored that small, panicky voice inside her. It would be, she told herself. She would make sure it was. She'd made her choice and she would enjoy every very pleasurable moment of it.

They drove down winding roads through ancient hill towns and sleepy villages until they came to a pair of impressive stone pillars topped with lions and a long sweeping drive that led to a sprawling whitewashed villa with a red-tiled roof, perched on its own hillside, surrounded by vineyards and olive groves.

'Alessandro!' An elegant yet relaxed-looking woman in her fifties with long, curly greying hair came out onto the steps as the car pulled up. 'I thought you weren't coming till tomorrow.'

'Change of plan.' Alessandro stepped out of the car and then extended a hand to Liane, keeping hold of it as he approached the woman and kissed her on both cheeks. '*Ciao*, Christina. Where's Sophia?'

'On her phone as usual, I'm sure,' Christina answered with a laugh. 'She'll be down in a second.' She glanced in curiosity at Liane. 'But who is this?'

Alessandro laced his fingers with hers as he drew Liane to his side. 'This,' he said firmly, 'is Liane.'

Liane didn't miss the note of possessive pride in his voice and she thought Christina didn't either, as a speculative gleam entered the older woman's eyes.

'I'm glad to meet you,' she said as a teenager tumbled out of the front door.

'Alessandro!' she exclaimed, and hurled herself into her half-brother's arms.

Liane took a step away, watching in poignant bemusement as Alessandro hugged the smiling, dark-haired girl. Here, she thought, was someone who loved him and wasn't afraid to show it. And he had to love her back, judging by the way he hugged her before he set her on her feet.

If he was capable of that kind of love...

No. She couldn't let herself think that way. Hope that much. She'd known what she was agreeing to when she'd said yes to Alessandro. Yes to a night, maybe two, perhaps even three, and no more. As long as she kept reminding herself of that, she'd be fine.

'Come inside,' Alessandro said, reaching for her hand once again. As he took it, Sophia's gaze narrowed and she glanced at Liane in unabashed curiosity, although without any hostility. Liane smiled, and Sophia smiled back.

Inside, the villa was an eclectic and tasteful mix of old world antiques and comfortable modern pieces. Christina led the way into a sprawling living room, its louvred doors open to an inner courtyard with orange trees and a tinkling fountain. A staff member brought iced coffees and a selection of Italian pastries.

'So...we've been watching your story unfold on social media,' Christina told them with a laugh as they sat down. 'Everyone's buzzing with it, wondering who your Princess is, Alessandro.' She gave him a teasing look. 'And now we know.' There was a slight questioning lilt to her voice and Liane forced herself to rush in.

'Oh, no. That was just a...a stunt, for publicity.'

'A stunt?' Christina glanced at Alessandro. 'That's not like you. You hate publicity.'

He shrugged, reaching for a pastry. 'The hotels had the publicity, not me.'

'So you don't mind that everyone is wondering what lovely young woman has caught your eye?'

'It was you, wasn't it,' Sophia interjected eagerly, 'running out of the ball last night? I saw it on YouTube this morning!'

She was on YouTube? Liane's stomach cramped. She wasn't ready to be famous, not even for fifteen minutes, and she definitely wasn't ready for her romance with Alessandro to be offered for public consumption. Except of course it wasn't a romance; it was an *arrangement*.

She wasn't having second thoughts, she told herself fiercely. She absolutely wasn't. She was looking forward to tonight; she was practically counting the minutes. Her body was still humming. And yet despite all that she still felt she had to brace herself for the hurt she knew would come after, no matter how hard she tried to avoid it.

'We came here to get away from all that,' Alessandro told his sister and former stepmother. 'We'd had enough of the speculation.'

'Our lips are sealed, then,' Christina replied, her eyes dancing. 'I'm glad you brought someone to meet me, at least.' She turned to Liane. 'He never has before, you know.'

'Oh…' Liane couldn't think of anything to say. She didn't want another reason to hope. 'I'm only staying for a day or two.' She glanced at Alessandro, whose bland gaze gave nothing away. 'Actually, I should call my sister, let her know where I am. Do you mind…?'

Christina gestured to the hall. 'Of course not. Please.'

Liane murmured her apologies as she rose from her seat and stepped out into the hall, wondering if Ella would even answer her call, yet feeling a sudden, desperate need to talk to her sister. To hear her advice, even if she'd never been brave enough before to follow it.

'Liane?' To her surprise, Ella picked up after the first ring. 'How are you?'

'Good. I think.'

'You think? What's going on with Alessandro? You guys didn't fight, did you? I saw the photo of you running out of the ballroom. I posted it this morning. People are going crazy.'

'You didn't!' Liane exclaimed. 'Has absolutely everyone seen that wretched photo?'

'About three hundred thousand people, last time I checked. What's going on?' Ella sounded surprisingly interested, even avid. 'Where are you?'

'I…that is, we…we decided not to go to Rome. I'm in Umbria, at Alessandro's family's villa.'

'Oh, I *see*.' Ella sounded delighted, and Liane let out an uncertain little laugh.

'Yes, I guess you do.'

'So you *are* having fun.'

'Well…' Liane did her best to ignore the fluttery panic taking up residence in her stomach. 'I hope to.'

'Ah, Liane!' Ella let out a throaty chuckle. 'That's the spirit! He's crazy about you, you know. Don't doubt it.'

'You drive me mad.'

But how had Ella been able to see that? 'Crazy about me for the moment,' she agreed, 'but that's all.'

'Then enjoy the moment,' Ella advised. 'And see what happens. Is it just the two of you?'

'No, his father's ex-wife and her daughter are here. Sophia. She's fourteen, and clearly adores her brother.'

'Sophia, hmm? I'm sure they'll both be eager to give you some privacy. Anyway, he adores *you*.'

'Ella! He doesn't.' Liane's face flushed and she lowered her voice, not wanting anyone to overhear. 'It's... it's not like that.'

'I wouldn't be so sure.'

'Trust me—'

'Oh, he might be fighting it, and you might be as well, but I know what I see.' She let out a peal of laughter. 'Social media doesn't lie.'

'Don't be ridiculous,' Liane protested. The last thing she wanted to think about was wretched social media. 'Anyway, I just called to tell you where I am.'

'Right. Well, I could have guessed that,' Ella told her loftily. 'Or at least who you were with. Keep me posted. And I mean that literally.'

'You seem happy, Alessandro.'

Alessandro turned to see his former stepmother glancing at him in gentle speculation. She'd been married to his father for only a handful of years before she'd left him because of his unfaithfulness, but she'd been pragmatic about the relationship, and grateful she'd got a daughter out of it. Even though she'd divorced his father over ten years ago, because of Sophia they'd remained close.

'I am,' he replied equably. Christina had shown Liane her room, with Sophia in tow, before returning downstairs to him.

'Because of her?' she asked, and he gave her a quelling look, or at least the approximation of one. In truth he was feeling too light and easy inside to get seriously annoyed with his stepmother's curious questions.

'Don't read more into it than there is,' he warned her. Even if he already felt the *more* in himself. His feelings for Liane went beyond the physical, he knew that much. 'We've only known each other a week, after all.' Could it really be such a short amount of time?

'Sometimes that's all it takes. I fell for your father in a single night.'

Alessandro's stomach tightened. He was *not* going to be like his father. 'And look how that turned out.'

'That may be, but I still loved him. Love doesn't follow rules, Alessandro.'

'This isn't love.'

'Are you sure?'

'Give it a rest, Christina.' He spoke good-naturedly although he was starting to feel tense. 'And don't push.'

'I won't,' she promised with a laugh. 'But it's nice to see you happy, with a woman. Sophia will be the one ringing the wedding bells for you. She can't wait to have a little niece or nephew.'

'Good Lord.' Alessandro shuddered, but there was more theatricality in it than conviction. He found himself picturing Liane's fairy tale garden, with the dogs and the cats and, yes, the children. 'I think I'll go see how Liane is settling in.'

His stepmother's laughter followed him out of the room. 'You do that,' she said.

Upstairs he found Liane perched on the window seat of her bedroom, with Sophia sprawled on her bed, her chin planted in her hands. Liane, he saw, was looking bemused, Sophia eager.

'So you've been to four balls together?'

'Well, not exactly together…' She glanced at Alessandro, who flicked his fingers at his half-sister.

'Out, scamp. I want to talk to Liane alone.'

Far from looking injured at being so dismissed, Sophia's face lit up. 'Of course you do,' she said as she scrambled off the bed.

Alessandro turned to Liane. Sophia hesitated by the doorway and he let out a good-natured groan. *'Sophia.'*

With a laugh she scampered from the room.

'It seems we haven't escaped the speculation here,' Liane said lightly as she turned to look out of the window.

'Naturally they're curious.'

'Your gardens are beautiful.'

He took a step towards her, his hands in his pockets. 'There's even lilac.'

She closed her eyes briefly. 'Don't, Alessandro.'

Surprised by her reaction, he put his hand on her shoulder. 'Don't what?'

'Don't… I don't even know…don't tease. Or warn. Or whatever it is you're doing. I know what this is. I'm perfectly fine with it, trust me.'

He pressed her shoulder gently to turn her towards him. 'And what is this?'

'An affair. One of your arrangements.' She drew an unsteady breath. 'I just want to be clear with you that I understand, so you don't have to keep giving me reminders. I'm not going to hope for or even think about more than...than what we have. I promise you I won't.'

Her words should have given him great relief, but he only felt disquiet. 'Is that supposed to reassure me?'

'Yes, of course it is.' A flash of something almost like ire was in her eyes. 'Why shouldn't it?' Indeed, that was the question, wasn't it? 'Anyway,' she dismissed, 'enough about that.'

Alessandro continued to gaze at her, noting the steely glint in her eye, the determined tilt of her chin. She'd made up her mind, without any regrets. He should be thrilled, he thought wryly. He had everything he'd wanted—Liane with him, agreeing to an affair, no strings, no complications. No possibility of either of them getting hurt.

So why did he feel so...strange?

'Why don't we go explore the garden?' he suggested. 'I want to show you the property.'

'All right.' The smile she gave him was both bright and determined. 'Let me just change.'

Fifteen minutes later they were strolling through the extensive gardens, past tinkling fountains and tumbling miniature waterfalls, climbing clematis and beds of sweet-smelling lavender. Liane had changed into a sundress in pale green linen, her hair in a single plait over one shoulder.

'So whose villa is this, anyway?' she asked as she bent to breathe in the fragrance of a deep pink over-blown rose.

'Mine. I bought it while I was working in Rome, as a bolthole, I suppose. Christina and Sophia were living in Milan then. Christina's British, as you might have guessed, but she was translating Italian textbooks for a living while she raised Sophia singlehandedly. When the rent got too expensive in the city, I offered for them to live here.'

Liane turned to him in surprise. 'Too expensive?'

'My father is perpetually broke,' Alessandro explained with a shrug. 'My grandfather knew him for a wastrel and so kept most of his assets in trust. He has enough to live in Ibiza, but not much to give to Christina, and so I've helped. Sophia is my sister, after all.'

'She's very sweet. Asking me all sorts of questions, though.'

Alessandro nodded in acknowledgement, a small smile tugging at his mouth. He'd always had a soft spot for his half-sister, wanting her to have the stability and love he hadn't known, even with her parents having divorced. 'She's a good kid.'

'She's lucky to have you. And this.' They'd strolled up to a lilac bush, its purple blossoms drooping nearly to the ground. With a small smile, Alessandro broke off a stem and handed it to her. Liane closed her eyes as she breathed in the scent. 'It smells like memory to me. There was a lilac bush outside our house in Lyon when I was growing up, during happier days.'

'Do you miss it?' Alessandro asked quietly.

'I miss the idea of it more than anything. A happy home. Two parents. My father wasn't gambling then. My mother wasn't quite so stern. We had a little dog, Bisou. It felt…simpler. It all changed when we moved to Paris for a bit, and then on to New York. After my father started gambling, he was never the same.' She sighed as she twirled the flower by its stem. 'Sometimes I wonder if the daydreams I've had are nothing more than me trying to get back what was lost. Maybe it's better, wiser, just to let it all go.'

'Don't say that.' He realised he couldn't stand the thought of her giving up on her dream—the garden, the cat and the dog, the children. 'It will happen for you.'

'Maybe,' she replied with a shrug, 'but what if it doesn't? Shouldn't I at least accept that might be the case?' Liane twirled the lilac blossom by its stem once more and then flung it onto a small pond nearby, where it floated, slightly bedraggled, on the water. 'Surely it's better to grab what you can of life, enjoy it while it lasts, than wait for a silly dream. That's why I'm here, after all.' She met his gaze with a playful smile.

'And I'm very glad you are.' He reached for her hand, drawing her to him.

As she came closer, her eyes fluttered closed and his lips brushed hers. 'I am too,' she whispered. 'Truly.'

He deepened the kiss, let it take them over. Liane wrapped her arms around him as she lost herself to the moment, just as he was—a moment that was as sweet as it was passionate, as innocent as it was sensual, her soft body yielding to his, promising so much.

As they drew apart, that was when it hit him.

All along he'd been insisting to himself that he would never be weak like his father, or needy like his mother. He wouldn't beg someone to stay; he wouldn't even want them to. He'd keep himself from dreams, from love, from hurt, taking each moment and enjoying life just as Liane had said…*except he hadn't.* All the while he'd been searching, longing, hoping. Feeling empty inside…until Liane.

And now, Alessandro thought as he stared down at her, the fairy tale had found him.

CHAPTER THIRTEEN

LIANE GAZED OUT at the violet night, the first stars beginning to twinkle in the night sky, and a shiver of expectation went through her as the cool breeze from the open shutters whispered over her skin.

She and Alessandro had spent the afternoon going through the garden and then playing a rollicking game of lawn boules with Sophia. Then they'd gathered in the drawing room for drinks, followed by a dinner that was both delicious and enjoyable, as Liane had seen how relaxed Alessandro was with the people he loved, smiling and joking in a way he had so rarely during their travels together.

And yet through it all an exquisite tension had been building inside her as well as between them. Every time she'd caught Alessandro's glance her body burned. When, during dinner, he'd casually brushed her fingers with his own everything in her had ached with desire. She'd enjoyed the towering sense of expectation, even as it had frightened her.

This was really happening...

As soon as dessert had been cleared, Christina and

Sophia had both made their excuses; Liane didn't miss the fact that her bedroom suite was in a guest wing, far from any others. Ella had been right; they were certainly giving her—them—privacy.

She'd returned to her room, showered and changed, feeling a bit self-conscious and even silly as she'd slipped on the thick terrycloth robe provided. Almost like a bride on her wedding night...except of course that wasn't how it was at all. And she didn't even know if or when Alessandro would arrive. Arrangement this might be, but they'd made no *actual* arrangements about how it was all supposed to go.

Should she go to his room? He to hers? How was this actually going to *work*?

She'd been standing at the window, trying not to let her nerves overwhelm her, for fifteen minutes before she heard the gentle tap at the door, and in the next moment Alessandro slipped into the room, regarded her with eyes that blazed silver with intensity—and desire.

He wore a white button-down shirt, open at his bronzed throat, and a pair of dark grey trousers. He looked so potently virile that Liane's heart turned over and a flush broke out over her skin. She felt, quite suddenly, nearly naked in her dressing gown and she fumbled with the sash to, rather ridiculously, tighten it.

'I didn't know if you were coming.'

He took a step towards her, a tiny, tender smile quirking his mouth. 'Why would you doubt it?'

'I don't know. Lack of experience, I suppose.'

'I've been thinking about this all day. For quite a few days, in fact.' Another step and another, and then he was there in front of her, gazing down at her with both tenderness and need. 'Surely you need no more convincing of how much I want you?'

'No...' she whispered. 'Although, to tell the truth, it does boggle my mind.'

He laughed softly. 'As it does mine.' He tugged gently on the end of her sash. 'Is there a reason why you were tightening that? You haven't changed your mind?'

'No.' She gulped. 'I was tightening it because right now you're wearing a few more clothes than I am,' she explained a bit tartly. 'And I'm nervous.' He smiled as he toyed with the end of her sash.

'The clothing situation can be remedied, you know. Quite quickly, as a matter of fact.'

'Okay.' She waited for him to unbutton his shirt, shrug out of it—*something*. But he merely looked at her. 'Would you do the honours?' he asked softly, and a nervous excitement skittered along her skin.

Could she...? Would she? Was that how this was going to work? Oh, yes, she realised, it was, and she would. Her fingers trembled at the first button, but by the third they were steady, and by the fourth they were lingering. His skin felt like burnished satin, the crisp hairs tickling her fingers, the muscles of his chest and abdomen tautening under her lightly skimming touch. Pleasure flared low in her belly as she undid the last button and then slid the shirt off his powerful shoulders.

He was so beautiful, every muscle sculpted in bronze, his taut belly quivering as she trailed her fingertips over it, and a low groan escaped him as he captured her fingers with his own.

'First let me look at you.'

With one slow tug he undid her robe and the heavy folds swung apart. Liane tried not to shiver, both from the cool air and the inevitable sense of apprehension as Alessandro regarded her naked body. She was too pale, too slight, Liane thought, even as she registered the gleam of deep masculine approval in his eyes.

He reached out one hand to cup her breast, his palm warm and sure, making her whole body tingle. 'You're perfect,' he told her. 'Absolutely perfect.'

And, amazingly, she *felt* perfect, in his eyes, in a way she never, ever had before. She finally felt seen and accepted and loved…yes, loved, even if she knew she wasn't, not like that. What she saw in his eyes, what she felt in herself, was, in that moment, enough. It was more than enough.

Her self-consciousness faded away as he slid the robe from her shoulders and it fell in a soft, silent pool at her feet. He took another step towards her so her breasts brushed his chest and everything in her quivered. A kiss, slow and deep, plumbing the very depths of her, and already she felt her mind start to blur and the last of her nervousness burned away in the heat of his gaze, as well as that of her desire, their bodies brushing each other at the most exquisitely aching points.

Boldly now, sure of his need as well as of her own, she reached for his belt buckle. Her fingers didn't tremble as she undid it and then the button on his trousers, her palm skimming the length and heat of him, thrilling to that touch, feeling him strain against her with desire and need. A slight smile of acknowledgement curved his mouth, the colour high on his cheekbones, his glittering gaze pinned on her. She didn't look away as, taking a steadying breath, she tugged his trousers down his muscular legs and then in one abrupt movement he kicked them off.

'And the rest?' he murmured and, taking a deep breath, she pulled his boxer shorts down, thrilling to the sight of his body, glorious and naked, ready for her.

In an instant they fell upon one another, bodies glimmering in moonlight, grasping, seeking, finding, hands and mouths, limbs tangled, a laugh escaping along with a groan, and Liane didn't even know who it was. It didn't even matter; she felt as if they were moving as one, a tangle and a blur as they stumbled their way to the bed, until, with a muttered oath, in one easy movement Alessandro swooped her into his arms and laid her down on it like a treasure, a precious pearl.

She gazed at him with nothing but trust in her eyes, her body utterly open to him, revelling in the desire and appreciation she saw in his heated gaze. Here she was, exposed, vulnerable, and yet not afraid. Not ashamed.

Then he stretched out beside her, one hand slowly skimming her body as if it learned its lines, from the curve of her ankle to the dip of her waist to the swell of her breast. A new country, explored by his hand—and then by his mouth as, with leisurely languor, he followed that route with his lips, seeming to memorise every hidden swell or dip until Liane was writhing beneath his questing touch, and wanting to explore his body in just the same way. To know him the way he was knowing her, for that was what it felt like—an intimacy beyond any other, a communion of bodies if not souls.

And yet already she knew her soul was touched, that no matter how she'd tried to separate it all in her mind, in reality the two were entwined for ever. She couldn't possibly separate her body from her heart; they were innately, intensely joined, just as their bodies were joining—Alessandro's leg between hers, his hands in her hair, his lips on her navel, making her gasp, dipping lower.

How could this be anything but a total offering of self, of soul—and a joining with his? Whether he knew it or not, whether she admitted it to him or not, Liane knew what this was—a total surrender, not just to him, but to what she felt for him. No matter how hard she'd tried to guard her heart, to keep it safe, she knew then that she'd offered it along with her body. She loved him and could not keep herself from loving him…whether or not he loved her back.

Had he ever felt this way before? Already Alessandro knew he had not. The physical transactions that had counted for his arrangements in the past, merely to satiate a physical need, had been nothing like this. They'd been nothing, full stop, forgotten in an instant, while Liane—her perfect body, her open, trusting gaze—would be seared on his memory for ever.

She lay supine beneath him, her expression dazed as

she gazed up at him in both wonder and need. A gasp escaped her as his mouth moved lower, testing, tasting. A shaky laugh as her fingers drove into his hair.

'Alessandro...'

He loved the way she said his name, with both wonder and need. He kissed his way lower, along her belly to her thighs, longing for her to say it again.

'Alessandro...'

The ache in her voice, the throb of her body...had he known anything sweeter? Deeper? She arched against him as he tasted her sweetness, his mouth hot and sure on her most intimate place, exploring the very depths of her, making her moan out as his own body throbbed with longing.

'Please...' she gasped as she thrust her hips up in instinctive demand. 'Please...'

He braced himself on his forearms as he gazed down at her flushed face. 'I'm trying to go slowly...' he told her, his teeth gritted from the effort of holding back, when all he wanted to do was plunge deep inside her and lose himself completely.

'Don't.' She let out an unsteady laugh as he reached for a condom. '*Don't.* I'll go mad...please... I want you inside me...completely.'

And then he was, a gasp escaping him as he felt her warmth enfold him, *accept* him. Accepting him completely. She folded her body around his, drew him even more deeply into herself, giving him all that she had.

'Oh...' she whispered, and then thrust up against him, her arms clasping him to her as her body instinctively began to move in that ancient rhythm, that beautiful dance. '*Oh*... I never knew...'

Neither had he. The sense of completion was far more than physical in that moment, as if they'd joined everything, and not just their bodies. Alessandro matched her pace, watched with a deep, primal satisfaction as her eyes widened and her lips parted and pleasure sang through their veins, united them in its joyous melody, taking them higher and higher, each note more beautiful than the last...

And then they arced on a crescendo of pleasure, their bodies trembling in the aftershocks as he clasped her against him, rolling onto his back and bringing her with him, never wanting to let her go. Ever.

He felt both broken open and made whole, as if it was in the breaking, the revealing, that he'd found something even more. It was as if his world had shifted on its axis and then righted, and he now saw it all so much more clearly than ever before.

Was this, then, what he'd been afraid of for so long? This startling clarity, as if the entire world had been brought into dazzling focus, and a deep, settled happiness thrummed through his veins. Was this what he'd been running away from?

Sex, for him, had always been about using—a pleasurable mutual using, but a using just the same. A transaction, a trade-off. This felt completely different, utterly more...instead of a deal, it had been a surrender. Instead of using, he had given.

It both humbled and amazed him, and horrified him too, because this was so new, so strange, and even with

Liane clasped in his arms he wasn't entirely sure he welcomed it.

Liane's body was boneless against his as she pressed her damp forehead against his shoulder.

'We are definitely doing that again before I go,' she told him, and Alessandro let out a huff of startled laughter before her words trickled through him.

Before I go? Her words sounded like a warning, and perhaps one he needed. She'd said such things before, but he'd thought they'd been for her own sake. Now he wondered if they were actually for his. Why should he assume that what he felt in this moment was real, or more than infatuation? Liane had no trouble making clear what she thought. She knew the rules—and so should he, because he'd made them. How could he let his judgement be so clouded?

He was acting like a lovesick fool, he realised with a burning twist of shame. Doing the exact thing he'd warned Liane against—reading so much more into a physical transaction that had been mind-blowingly pleasurable…and no more.

And yet it *had* felt like more…for him. And the thought was as terrifying as it was wonderful. He didn't want this—the risk, the pain, the rejection, the fear. *The joy.* He didn't want to love Liane—and yet he was afraid he did.

The fairy tale might have come for him after all, but had it for her?

The question was still thudding through him as she slipped out of his arms, off the bed, and disappeared into the bathroom. Alessandro felt the yawning absence in his empty arms, the expanse of rumpled sheets. Quickly he disposed of the condom and moved to a seated position, raking a hand through his dampened hair. He'd felt as if he could have lain there for ever, sated and sleepy, but perhaps it was better this way. Get things back on the terms he was used to, the ones Liane had agreed to, and stop wondering if his world had changed when it hadn't.

It was another five minutes before she returned, looking cool and composed. She walked over to the crumpled heap of her dressing gown and shrugged it on.

'What now?' she asked with a small, rueful smile, or at least an attempt at one. 'I'm afraid I don't know the rules. Do we sit and chat? Do you go back to your room?'

He almost smiled at her practical tone, even as it stung. He didn't know the rules either, not any more, and though he knew he should remind himself of them, he didn't. He knew what he wanted—Liane in his bed, for the rest of the night.

'Now you take off that ridiculous dressing gown and come back to bed,' Alessandro told her. 'And we stay here till morning.'

Her playful smile turned cautious, surprised. 'Till morning?'

'Yes. Till morning. At the very least.' He held his arms out and with a little laugh she shrugged off the robe once again and scrambled across the bed towards him.

Laughing too, Alessandro snatched her up in his

arms, rolled her under him as she squirmed breathlessly, looking up at him with both joy and wonder.

'I thought…' she began, and he silenced her with a kiss.

'No thinking,' he told her as his mouth moved lower. 'No thinking at all.'

He wasn't going to think about what this was, not now. There would be time later to worry, to wonder, because all he wanted now was the sweetness of Liane in his arms, looking up at him, giving herself to him. Again and again.

CHAPTER FOURTEEN

THE NEXT WEEK passed in a golden haze of happy moments. Not for the first time since meeting Alessandro Rossi, Liane wondered if she should pinch herself. It certainly felt as if she were dreaming.

They spent the days lazing in the garden or villa, walking through the hills or wandering through the sun-soaked towns, playing boules or cards or taking a dip in the pool. Sophia often accompanied them, developing a friendship with Liane as she watched her easy camaraderie with Alessandro. Christina worked from home during the day, although she joined them in the evenings for dinner, with laughter and conversation, sometimes long into the night, although never too long, leaving Alessandro and Liane plenty of time together.

'Sophia is thrilled to have Alessandro here for so long,' she told Liane one evening, while they were waiting for the others to join them in the drawing room. 'He usually only stays for a day or two, and it's been a whole week.'

'Has it?' Liane felt as if the days had flown, each one more precious than the last, for who knew when they would end? She'd told herself—and Ella, when she'd texted to check in—that she was simply enjoying letting it all happen, the moments as they came, and she was, oh, she *was*.

For beyond the fun-filled days there were the pleasure-filled nights…as night after night she and Alessandro explored each other's bodies, drove each other to new heights of both passion and intimacy, limbs tangled, hands seeking, hearts thudding as one.

Could you *do* those things with someone, Liane had wondered more than once, and not fall in love with them? She was already realising, more and more with each passing day, she couldn't. With every day she spent with Alessandro she fell deeper and deeper in love. She'd even stopped trying to keep herself from it, knowing there was no use, and understanding for the first time why Ella was so willing to tumble headlong into relationships.

It was *fun*. It was wonderful to look at someone and have your stomach fizz, your heart fill. To lie in someone's arms and listen to the thud of their heart, to roll over and see the smile playing on their lips as they drew you closer for a kiss. To feel that closely attuned, that dearly beloved.

Was there anything more wonderful, more magical, than falling in love?

Well, yes, Liane knew there was. It was knowing that person loved you back.

Sometimes, when she caught Alessandro looking at her, or when he held her in his arms and stroked her hair after they'd made love, both of their hearts still racing as the aftershocks of their climax shuddered through them, she could almost convince herself that he did. Or at least, perhaps, that he could, if he let himself. He was capable of it, surely; whether he was willing was another matter.

Sometimes, as they wandered through the market of a nearby hill town, buying a jar of olives swimming in brine and a crusty loaf of bread for an impromptu picnic, she told herself it didn't matter if he loved her or not. This was enough—his attention, his affection, his body in her bed. Did she really need more than that? Wasn't she happy enough, at least for now?

Then she'd catch him looking pensive, a shadow coming over his face as he became remote, and it felt like the sun disappearing behind the clouds, a darkness coming over the whole earth. His answers would become clipped, his gaze distant, and her heart would thud an erratic beat as she wondered if he was thinking of ending it between them. She thought she saw it in the tightening of his mouth, the flicker in his eyes, and a few times she felt he'd been on the cusp of saying something. *It's been fun, but...*

It had been longer than she'd expected, she knew, longer than she'd even hoped. She shouldn't, she told herself, even be surprised. Really, she should be ready.

In those moments she knew she couldn't live in the balance, always wondering, worrying what would come next. She might not crave the spotlight, but she no longer wanted to live in the shadows. Not like that, anyway. If he couldn't love her, it would be better to end it, surely.

And yet...they'd only known each other a handful of weeks. Couldn't she give him time to develop the feelings she knew she already had? If he could just tell her he wanted to *try*...

But he never did.

Ten days into their idyll, seeming more remote than ever, he shut himself away in his study for most of the afternoon and Liane half wondered if she should pack her bags. She gazed out at the lemony sunlight spilling over the gardens and hated the thought of leaving this wonderful place where she'd briefly known so much happiness. But perhaps it would be better to leave before Alessandro told her to...if she had the strength. Was that what was going to happen?

Wouldn't she rather be the first to say, *It was fun, but...?* A sense of self-preservation told her she would, and yet even so she was reluctant. She wasn't ready to say goodbye...

Just then her phone buzzed with a call from Ella.

'So, it's been ten days,' she said by way of greeting. 'Are you guys engaged yet or what?'

'Ella!' Liane couldn't keep from sounding horrified. What if Alessandro overheard? Not, of course, that he would. He was still holed up in his study, ignoring her. 'Don't talk like that, please. As a matter of fact, I was just thinking about whether I should go home.'

'What?' Ella sounded shocked. 'Why?'

'To keep myself from getting hurt,' Liane stated flatly. *It was too late for that, though, wasn't it?* 'Alessandro said this would end when he said it would,' she told Ella. 'And I'd like to think I have a little more self-respect than to wait for him to tell me to go.'

'He's not going to end it,' Ella insisted. 'He loves you.'

'Ella, we've only known each other for a couple of weeks,' Liane reminded her painfully. 'And I'm not sure Alessandro even knows what love is, or, more importantly, if he wants to. He's told me he doesn't, as a matter of fact.'

'That may be true,' Ella answered slowly, 'but maybe he needs someone to point it out to him.'

'And you think I should?' The thought terrified her. If she told him she loved him and he rejected her, and he *would* reject her, surely… There was a reason why she stayed in the shadows, wasn't there? The spotlight was far too bright, too dangerous. 'I don't know if I can do that.'

'I'm not sure you should at this point,' Ella replied thoughtfully. 'I think he actually needs to see it for himself.'

'How?' Liane cried. If only it were simply a matter of *seeing*…

'I know how.' Ella sounded alarmingly certain.

'You do?' Liane exclaimed. 'Ella, don't even think of… I don't even know what. But don't.'

Ella only laughed. 'What could I really do from France?' she asked innocently.

'I don't know, but please—'

'Sometimes,' Ella cut across her, 'love needs a little helping hand. Or at least a mirror.'

And with that she hung up, leaving Liane both fuming and afraid, wondering what on earth Ella could be up to now. But did it really matter? Would Ella's interference, whatever it was and no matter how well meaning, make a difference to Alessandro's feelings? To his heart?

Liane glanced out at the gardens, now gilded in evening sunlight; from the open window she breathed in the faint fragrance of lilac. The flowers she loved so much, she'd seen earlier that day, were browning at the edges, their blooms already fading, releasing the last of their sweet, sweet scent, as the season turned and summer came on with its relentless heat and endless blue skies.

Maybe that was just how life happened; one season gave birth to another. She and Alessandro had had something special, but that was all it was—a season, a moment in time. Perhaps she was foolish in longing for it to be more. To wish for the fairy tale...

And yet why shouldn't she at least *try*? Perhaps she was stubborn, or merely hopeful, but she wanted to be brave enough to tell him how she felt, or at least how she *thought* she felt. It was all still so new, she could admit that, but it was still something... Maybe, just maybe, she could be brave enough to step into the spotlight once more.

The tap at the door had Alessandro looking up from his desk in weary irritation. He'd spent the last eight hours trying to put out the flames of a scandal that had been brewing while he'd been essentially asleep at the wheel.

One of their investors whose fund they managed

had been caught with his hand in the cookie jar, to the tune of many millions, and there were those who were looking to implicate Rossi Enterprises as well.

'You know that saying, no publicity is bad publicity?' one of his staff had remarked tiredly. 'Well, that's certainly not the case.'

No, it wasn't. Alessandro hadn't paid any attention to the media in the last ten days, but now he saw that the financial scandal was splashed all over the newspapers and some smart aleck had decided to tie the breaking scandal to his appearance at the Rossi balls. *Is the Prince of Manhattan too busy playing with his Princess to pay attention?* ran one headline. Another one screamed *Notorious recluse has decided the party circuit is more fun than fusty numbers...*

For heaven's sake. Once upon a time such things would have coldly amused him, for he knew absolutely that they held no truth. Now, he wondered. Why had he allowed himself to get so distracted? He'd never been away from the office for this long. He'd never spent days ignoring the world around him for the woman right there. *What was happening to him?*

Was it love—a thought that admittedly terrified him—or merely infatuation? The prospect made him feel bleak. How could he know? How could he trust himself, never mind Liane? *And did he even want to?*

'Alessandro?' Liane's voice was soft, tentative.

Alessandro raked his hands through his hair as he pushed himself away from the desk. 'Come in.'

She opened the door cautiously, standing in the

doorway as she regarded him with dark, uncertain eyes. 'You've been working?'

'Yes.' He paused. 'I'm sorry I haven't been available.'

'It's all right. I never expected...' She swallowed. 'I understand you have other obligations.'

She sounded so small and sad, and it filled Alessandro with both remorse and annoyance. He didn't want to care so much...and yet he did.

'I just...' She swallowed hard, her face flushing, her hands clasped together tightly. 'I know you're busy, and maybe...maybe you need to return to Rome or New York or wherever...'

'What are you saying?' His voice came out terse.

'I just wanted to tell you that I...that I've really...'

The *ping* from his mobile lying on the desk made her falter and Alessandro's gaze snapped to the screen, which was lighting up with message after message.

Ping. Ping. Ping.

He snatched up the phone, swiping the screen, his eyes first widening and then narrowing as he read all the alerts.

'Alessandro...' Liane's voice wavered. 'What is it?'

His stomach clenched and he felt as if he'd swallowed a stone as he swiped through the images, one after the other: *The secret is out...the Prince of Manhattan is desperately in love!*

He looked up to see Liane, her face now deathly pale, biting her lips in nervousness. *I just wanted to tell you...*

'You did this?' he asked in a low voice.

She glanced nervously at the phone still clenched in his hand. 'Did what?'

'Put our...our *arrangement* up for public consumption.' He flung the word at her like a weapon, meant to wound. 'Were you hoping to force my hand? Did you actually think that would work?'

'I...' She shook her head slowly. 'What are you talking about?'

'You must know what I'm talking about.' No matter how innocent or confused she pretended to be. How else could these photos have been posted online? She must have been conspiring with Ella all along. The thought made him feel sick.

'Did Ella post something?' she asked, and he was reminded of the first night he'd seen her, when she'd come outside and recognised that damned shoe. He saw the flicker of recognition, resignation, in her eyes and he understood. She had known then, and she clearly knew now. Had their time together all been an act, a con? No, surely not. *And yet...*

'She might have posted it, but you provided the images.' Images of him that he'd never, ever want anyone to see.

'What images? Alessandro, I haven't seen anything—'

'Then go look on your phone,' he practically snarled. 'And then you can leave this house immediately.'

Even as he said the words he knew he didn't mean them. He was angry but, more fundamentally, he was hurt, devastated by her betrayal, and he was lashing out because he couldn't bear her to see his vulnerability, not when he'd been so used. Used in a way he'd promised himself he never would be, trotted out to serve someone else's schemes. Hers or Ella's, did it even matter? She'd been party to it all.

Liane's face was white, her eyes wide and dark as she stared at him. For a second he thought she'd walk out without a word, turn and run, an admission of guilt. Then colour flared in her cheeks and her eyes narrowed, her lips parting.

'So that's it, is it?' she asked with a strangely lethal quiet. 'You act as judge and jury? This is you deciding when it ends?' Her voice remained quiet yet it held a razor-sharp mocking edge that made Alessandro blink.

'I decide,' he replied, 'because of what you did.'

'I don't even know what I'm supposed to have done, but it doesn't even matter. Ella posted something. I get it. Just like I get how angry you are, because it's easier to be angry than hurt, isn't it, Alessandro? Be outraged and then you have a reason for running away.' She lifted her chin, her eyes glittering. 'I came down here to tell you I loved you. Or at least that I could love, if we had more time. If we gave ourselves that chance. Even though I was terrified, I was going to be brave enough to do it, to risk my heart and my pride, because I thought we shared something that was worth that risk. I thought—I deluded myself, really—that I could make you see that. Because...' her voice wavered and she took a quick steadying breath '...you made me feel *seen*. And important. And...and loved, in a way no one else had before. And I believed in that. I believed in us. More fool me, clearly.'

Alessandro opened his mouth but no words came out. He was reeling and yet he was still angry. 'Then who took these photos, Liane?' he demanded, and it wasn't until he'd spoken that he realised that wasn't the question he'd wanted to ask at all. *Do you really love me?* was the one that burned on his lips.

'Oh, Alessandro.' Liane gave a sad little laugh as she shook her head. 'I haven't even seen the photos, so I couldn't tell you. But it doesn't really matter, does it? For you to jump to the conclusion that I took them... and then to ask me to leave...' She drew a hitched breath. 'Well, that says it all, doesn't it? Unfortunately.' She paused, her spine straightening, that poignant lift of her chin. 'Thank you for these last few weeks. I'll go pack my bags.'

And he watched her walk out of the room, her back straight and proud, her body bristling with dignity, while he stayed silent.

CHAPTER FIFTEEN

She made it back to her bedroom before the tears came in a hot, scalding rush as she closed the door behind her and crumpled into a heap right there on the floor. *Stupid,* she thought. *Stupid, stupid, stupid. You knew all along he wasn't going to love you.*

But to *accuse* her, and of something so absurd—as if she would have taken photos and posted them…! It was an excuse, it had to be, or maybe he really didn't know her at all, much less love her…

Either way, did it really matter? He still wanted her gone.

Drawing a shuddering breath, Liane stood and walked on shaky legs to the wardrobe, resolutely pulling her suitcase out as an unruly sob escaped her. She'd call for a taxi, she'd leave right away. She couldn't bear seeing him again, that haughty look of disdain on his face…

From the bedside table, her phone pinged. She didn't even want to look at the photos Ella must have posted, although she supposed she ought at least to know what had been the catalyst for her heartbreak. Sniffing, she pushed her tangled hair out of her face and went to grab her phone.

It only took a few swipes to get to Ella's profile and then a shuddery breath escaped her as she slowly lowered herself onto the edge of the bed. Silently she began to swipe through the photos—about a dozen—together, all of them telling a story. *Revealing the truth?*

No, not the truth. The truth, Liane acknowledged hollowly, was Alessandro's icy rage of just a few moments ago as he'd told her, just as he'd said he would, when their *arrangement* would end. And yet…she'd always known Ella was a master of manipulation, capturing the perfect image, zooming in on a face, spinning a story, just as she'd promised when Alessandro had first suggested she accompany him to all the Rossi hotels.

The Prince finds his Princess, indeed.

And what happened next?

He booted her out.

And yet here was the love story Ella had been wanting to tell—Alessandro gazing at Liane across the ballroom, his forehead wrinkled with concern, a faraway look in his eyes, with the caption underneath, *Looking for his Princess…* And there he was dancing with her, except the camera had zoomed in on Alessandro's face, and the unmistakably tender look softening his eyes, his mouth.

Liane gulped. There was more, so much more. Alessandro and her chatting on the plane, but again the camera revealed something Liane hadn't seen. The blatant look of affection in his eyes, the smile tugging at his mouth, the way his arm was draped across the top of her seat...

A gasp escaped her as she saw the next photo—of them kissing in the garden here at the villa, in what she'd believed to be a completely private moment. Who on earth could have taken that one? And another, walking hand in hand as the sun set behind them, through an olive grove. Liane was laughing as she looked up at him and Alessandro was smiling. There were several more, all taken at the villa, all showing a man who looked so wonderfully in love, showing the most vulnerable part of himself—to the world.

So this was what Ella had meant about giving a helping hand! But where on earth had she got the photos from? And then realisation thudded through her—Sophia. *Of course.* Ella must have contacted her through social media, enlisted her help. Sophia had been so cheerful, always popping up to spend time with them, always with her phone, as any teenager was...

A choked laugh escaped Liane that ended in a wavery sigh. Her sister had meant well, and so had Sophia, of that she was sure, but their so-called help had had the utterly opposite effect. Alessandro was more determined than ever not to believe the truth in these photos and to convict her instead of some sort of cold-hearted manipulation.

With another shuddery sigh she put the phone down. She had more sympathy for him now that she'd seen the photos, and she realised how hard they must have hit him. It must have been extremely galling—humiliating, even—for Alessandro to see those photos of himself looking so vulnerable, so open, his emotions seemingly laid bare, and especially when they'd been taken here, where he'd assumed it was private. He'd thought he was safe. For him to believe he was being used, just as he had been as a child...well, for him it was proof that the fairy tale wasn't real, wasn't it?

And it *wasn't*. Because, as compelling as these photos were, they weren't the truth. The truth was Alessandro coldly telling her to get out of his house, refusing even to listen to her. She'd done all she could, Liane knew. She'd told him she loved him. It might have been said in anger and hurt, but she'd meant it. All that was left now was to go.

And so she did, as quietly and unobtrusively as she did everything else—packing her single suitcase, calling a taxi, writing a note for Sophia and Christina thanking them for their hospitality, and then slipping out of the villa without anyone even noticing she had gone.

Half an hour later she was in Perugia; she took a connecting flight to Milan, spending the night in a cheap hotel, and then the next day flew back to New York, all in a state of numb, abject desolation.

By the time she arrived at the townhouse overlooking Central Park her eyes were gritty, her heart still aching. Twenty-four hours hadn't helped her feel the tiniest bit better. If anything, she felt worse, the loss of Alessandro reverberating emptily through her. She hadn't answered Ella's calls, simply texting her that she was going home. Then she'd turned off her phone because she knew she didn't want to deal with the media frenzy that had erupted with Ella's posts. If anything, she thought wearily as she lugged her suitcase up the steps of her home, she just wanted to go back to the way she had been before, safe in the shadows. The online world would forget her in a heartbeat, she knew. And so would Alessandro…

The front door opened and she glanced up, expecting to see her mother's stern face.

'I've been waiting for you.'

Liane's jaw dropped and her fingers slipped from the handle of her suitcase. *'Alessandro…'*

It had taken Alessandro about fifteen minutes to realise he was a complete idiot. He'd gazed at those photos, every single one, first in shock, then in shame, then in wonder. He hated, absolutely hated, feeling so exposed, his most private and personal emotions on display for everyone to see, and he hated even more the thought that Liane might have done it on purpose, aiding and abetting Ella in whatever publicity scheme they'd worked up.

He'd sat slumped in his chair for at least an hour, looking at those photos in turn as understanding had slowly crept up on him, like the dawn of a new morning. Of course Liane hadn't taken them on purpose. He doubted she'd even known they were being taken. He'd accused her out of anger and fear, not wanting to acknowledge the truth that was blazing out of each and every photo. The truth that he loved her.

He hadn't been able to deny it, even though his first instinct, as ever, had been to do just that. To accuse rather than admit. To lash out rather than love. When Sophia had come in tearfully a little while later, telling him Liane had already left and it was all her fault, Alessandro had been able to piece the story together. Ella had contacted Sophia, asked her to take some photos for her to use on her social media. Sophia had been thrilled, especially as she was so sure Alessandro and Liane were in love.

'But she's left and it's all my fault. I didn't realise how it would affect her...'

'It's not your fault, Sophia, *cara*,' Alessandro had told her grimly. 'It's mine.'

He was the prize idiot who could look love right in the face and pretend he wasn't seeing it. Love wasn't blind; *he* was. By the time he'd realised the truth Liane had already left. Alessandro had packed his bag within minutes and he'd been in a car to the private jet still idling in Perugia so fast his head spun.

'What are you doing here?' Liane asked now as he stood in the doorway of her house, shaking her head at him in weary wonder. 'And how did you get here before me?'

'Private jet, remember,' he replied with a little smile. His heart ached to see how tired and worn down she looked, how *sad*, sorrow shadowing her eyes and causing the corners of her mouth to droop. That was his fault. 'I arrived several hours ago.'

'I'm sorry about the photos,' Liane blurted. 'Ella must have arranged it all. She hinted to me that she was doing something, but I had no idea what. I could have guessed, I suppose, although I never thought she'd get Sophia involved...at least, I assume it was Sophia.'

'I don't care about the photos,' Alessandro assured her. Only to amend, 'Actually, I do care about the photos. Because they showed me something I should have been able to realise on my own—and I *did* realise it, but I fought against it because I was scared. Terrified, in fact.'

Hope started to spark in Liane's eyes and her lips trembled. 'Terrified...?' she whispered.

'Of love,' he stated starkly. His heart beat with painful thuds; as sure as he was, this still felt hard. Being vulnerable got easier, but perhaps it was never easy. Saying how you felt, admitting the truth. Being willing to be rejected. 'Of loving you. It wasn't until I saw those photos that I realised the truth of it. I couldn't deny it any longer, even though I tried, terribly. I'm so sorry for accusing you, Liane. For hurting you. I did it out of my own fear and hurt, but that is no excuse.' He reached for her hand, threading her fingers through his. 'Forgive me?'

Tears pooled in her eyes and she blinked them back rapidly. 'Oh, Alessandro...'

'I love you, Liane.' Instead of making him feel weak, as he'd always thought, saying it aloud made him feel strong. Powerful. 'You've made me believe in the fairy tale. You *are* the fairy tale. Or at least we can be it, together. We can try...not for some absurd photo op. Not for online consumption. But for us.'

His fingers tightened on hers as she gazed at him in both wonder and hope. 'I can't believe...'

'I couldn't either. I didn't want to. Love, to me, was about using and being used. Being hurt, being disappointed, being out of control. I let my parents' terrible marriage influence me—not just how they treated each other, but how they treated me, stuck in the middle, being used for their ends. I promised myself I'd never let myself need or be needed like that because it only ended in tears and regret. And yet, since meeting you, I've realised that that is a terrible way to live. Empty.'

A shaky laugh escaped her as she clasped their joined hands with her other. 'Well, it's certainly a lonely way. But I… I don't need the fairy tale, Alessandro. I just want real life…with you. I spent too long waiting to be swept away, telling myself it would happen without me needing to try. Waiting for my Prince to come charging down on his steed—'

'And meanwhile he stepped on your toes.'

She laughed, a pure, joyous sound. 'And charmed me while doing it.' She shook her head slowly. 'I still can't believe you're actually here. That you're saying these things.'

'I am here, my *bella* Liane,' he told her as he gathered her in his arms. 'Telling you I love you, now and for ever…if you'll have me.'

'I will,' she answered with heartfelt fervour and finally, thankfully, he kissed her.

EPILOGUE

Three years later

THE VILLA WAS swarming with stylists, models and photographers, all determined to create the perfect photo opportunity for Ella Ash's new fashion line, Cinders. After deciding social influencing was a bit too much like playing fairy godmother, Ella had gone into designing her own clothes, a mixture of frivolous and fun. She was an up-and-coming designer, considered 'the one to watch' by many fashion magazines, and when she'd asked Liane if she could have her first photo shoot at the villa in Umbria, Liane had told Alessandro and he'd laughingly rolled his eyes.

'We have to say yes, don't we?'

'Considering she brought us together,' Liane replied diplomatically, her eyes sparkling, 'I think so.'

'As long as she doesn't turn Emilia's head—'

'Emilia is two years old,' Liane reminded him with a laugh. 'I think she's a little young to be influenced by fashion and celebrity, although she does like sparkles.'

'Just like her mother then, with her ridiculous shoes.'

Now, as they gazed out at the garden, Alessandro slipped an arm around her waist as Liane stood on her tiptoes for the kind of kiss she never tired of. The last three years had been the happiest of her life; they'd split their time between Paris, Rome and the villa in Umbria, until Emilia was born and they'd moved there permanently. Liane was attempting a new translation of Victor Hugo's poetry while also caring for their daughter—and now another baby on the way, just a gentle bump beneath her flowing dress, a promise in the making.

She glanced around the villa's gardens, various assistants and stylists scuttling here and there. They'd put the dogs in the kitchen—they had two—and their cat had just had kittens. On each of their anniversaries Alessandro had planted a lilac bush, until Liane had teased him that they would be overtaken—not that she minded. It was all she'd dreamed of and more, better than any fairy tale she could have dreamed up.

Not, she reflected as Emilia came running over to them and Alessandro scooped her up in his arms, hoisted her on his shoulders, that there hadn't been challenges along the way as they'd come to know each other better, love each other more, because there had, but they'd been ones they'd faced together.

The fairy tale *wasn't* a fairy tale, Liane reflected. It was real and messy and wonderful and hard, all at once. It was life…together.

'Hey,' Ella called as she practically bounced up to them, brandishing her phone. 'We're almost ready and you guys look so perfect…' Liane glanced at Alessandro while he grimaced good-naturedly, tickling Emilia to make her laugh, and Ella, grinning, held her phone aloft.

'Now smile!'

* * * * *

If you couldn't put A Scandal Made at Midnight *down, then you're guaranteed to enjoy these other Kate Hewitt stories!*

Greek's Baby of Redemption
Claiming My Bride of Convenience
The Italian's Unexpected Baby
Vows to Save His Crown
Pride & the Italian's Proposal

Available now!

WE HOPE YOU ENJOYED
THIS BOOK FROM
✦ HARLEQUIN
PRESENTS

Escape to exotic locations where passion knows no bounds.

Welcome to the glamorous lives of royals and billionaires, where passion knows no bounds. Be swept into a world of luxury, wealth and exotic locations.

8 NEW BOOKS AVAILABLE EVERY MONTH!

COMING NEXT MONTH FROM

H HARLEQUIN

PRESENTS

#4025 THE BILLIONAIRE'S BABY NEGOTIATION
by Millie Adams
Innocent Olive Monroe has hated Icelandic billionaire
Gunnar Magnusson for years...and then she discovers the
consequences of their electric night together. Now she's facing
the highest-stakes negotiation of all—Gunnar wants their baby,
her company and Olive!

#4026 MAID FOR THE GREEK'S RING
by Louise Fuller
Achileas Kane sees himself as living proof that wedding vows are
meaningless. But this illegitimate son can only gain his inheritance
if he weds. His proposal to hotel chambermaid Effie Price is simply
a contract—until they seal their contract with a single sizzling kiss...

#4027 THE NIGHT THE KING CLAIMED HER
by Natalie Anderson
King Felipe knows far too much about the scandalous secrets in
Elsie Wynter's past. But with her stranded in his palace for one
night only, and their mutual desire flaring, he can think of nothing
but finally claiming her...

#4028 BOUND BY A NINE-MONTH CONFESSION
by Cathy Williams
Celia is unprepared for the passion she finds with billionaire
Leandro, let alone finding herself holding a positive pregnancy
test weeks later! Now they have nine months to decide if their
connection can make them a family.

#4029 CROWNING HIS KIDNAPPED PRINCESS
Scandalous Royal Weddings
by Michelle Smart

When daring Prince Marcelo Berruti rescues Clara Sinclair from a forced wedding, he makes international headlines. Now he's facing a diplomatic crisis...unless he claims the beautiful bride-to-be himself!

#4030 DESTITUTE UNTIL THE ITALIAN'S DIAMOND
by Julia James

Lana can't believe the crushing debts her ex left her with are forcing her to make a convenient marriage with ruthless Italian Salvatore. But while her head agrees to take his name, her body craves his forbidden touch!

#4031 INNOCENT IN HER ENEMY'S BED
by Dani Collins

Ilona is aware that Leander will do anything for revenge against her stepfamily. She just never pictured herself becoming his ally. Or that the sensual back-and-forth between them would lead to their marriage bed...

#4032 HIS DESERT BRIDE BY DEMAND
by Lela May Wight

Desert prince Akeem wants to show first love Charlotte what she gave up by turning her back on him. Then their secret tryst threatens to become a scandal, and duty-bound Akeem must make an outrageous demand: she'll be his queen!

YOU CAN FIND MORE INFORMATION ON UPCOMING HARLEQUIN TITLES, FREE EXCERPTS AND MORE AT HARLEQUIN.COM.

HPCNMRB0622

"Can you explain what happened?" Akeem asked. "The
intensity?"

Could she? Nine years had passed between them—a
lifetime—and still… No, she couldn't.

"My father had a lifetime of being reckless for his own
amusement—"

"And you wanted a taste of it?"

"No," he denied, his voice a harsh rasp.

"Then what did you want?" Charlotte pushed.

"A night—"

"You risked your reputation for a night?" She cut him
off, her insides twisting. "And so far, it's been a disaster,
and we haven't even got to bed." She blew out a puff of
agitated air.

"Make no mistake," he warned, "things have changed."

"Changed?"

"My bed is off-limits."

She laughed, a throaty gurgle. "How dare you pull me from my life, fly me who knows how many miles into a kingdom I've never heard of and turn my words back on me!" She fixed him with an exasperated glare. "How dare you try to turn the tables on me!"

"If the tables have turned on anyone," he corrected, "it is me because you will be my wife."